Tales From Toonopolis

Volume One

by
Jeremy Rodden

Internal Illustrations & Back Cover Illustration
by Cami Woodruff
Front Cover Illustration by Mel Tillery

Published by Portmanteau Press LLC, Chesapeake, VA

Published by:
Portmanteau Press LLC
PO BOX 1411
Chesapeake, VA 23327
http://www.portmanteaupress.com/

ISBNs: 978-0-9834253-5-9 (paperback), 978-0-9834253-7-3 (eBook)

Cover art and design by:
Mel Tillery
http://www.cyaneus.com/
& Cami Woodruff
http://www.camiwoodruff.com/

To the anthology publishers of 2017-2019 who gave me the encouragement to continue writing stories: Valerie, P.K., Heidi, Sammy, Mary, Paige, and Tara!

Contents

Preface

When I first published *Anchihiiroo – Origin of an Antihero* in 2011, just seven months after the release of *Toonopolis: Gemini*, the first *Toonopolis Files* book, I had people ask why it wasn't available in print. I told them that I had plenty of short stories and novellas in the tank and I'd compile them once I had enough for a book.

Fast forward nearly eight years, and *Tales from Toonopolis: Volume One* is here. In addition to the first "side story" for characters met in the main *Toonopolis Files* books, I have compiled four short stories that have been published in various anthologies over the years and the

steampunk novella *Misanthrope Beechworth &
The Dustwaste Wellspring*.

For the two novellas, this is the first
time they are available in print format.
For the rest, this is the first time they
exist in a "Toonopolis-only" collection!
All in all, I am excited to present *Tales
from Toonopolis Volume One* and have a
whole lot more Toonopolis stories to
share.

I hope you enjoy!

Jeremy Rodden

February 2019

Where Do Our Ideas Go?

Author Note:

This first story is a piece of flash fiction that was written on the now-defunct Authonomy forums. It features the kangaroo-duck mentioned in the first chapter of *Toonopolis: Gemini* where the concept of creation impermanence was first established in the Tooniverse.

It was first published in a charity anthology entitled A World of Their Own in September 2015 by Kristell Inklings. It was edited by A.F.E. Smith.

** 3 **

One of Juan Hernandez's favorite activities was sitting at his kitchen table while drinking his morning coffee and watching his four-year-old son Carlos draw pictures. Carlos had a fascinating imagination for such a young child and would often try to copy the cartoon characters he would see on television. Lately, Carlos had even begun making up his own creations.

Juan took a sip of his coffee and watched his son's idea come to life on the paper. The creature had the bill of a duck but long ears that didn't fit. After Carlos drew the webbed feet, he penciled a long, curved tail. Juan felt his eyebrows meet in the middle of his forehead as he tried to sort out what his son was creating. Carlos was clearly oblivious to his father's ponderings as he went to work drawing a large sombrero and a vest on the duck-type invention.

"What are you drawing, son?"

Without looking up, Carlos answered, "It's a kangaroo-duck, papi." The boy put down his pencil and reached for a yellow crayon, supplying the kangaroo-duck with color on the hat and vest. In a strange sort of way, the animal reminded Juan of The Man In The Yellow Hat from the *Curious George* books.

His son's intensity and focus on the drawing were more amazing than the drawing itself. Trying to get a four-year-old to sit still for more than a few minutes at a time was a challenge, but Carlos would sit and draw for hours.

Juan wondered where these ideas came from.

What he should have been wondering was where they go.

* * *

A kangaroo-duck popped into existence in a grassy field. The hybrid animal quickly assessed his surroundings. On the horizon, he saw a whole bunch of buildings and a sun shining brightly above them. The sun had a face on it. To many people, this would seem strange. The kangaroo-duck, though, had only existed for a short period of time so had no basis for comparing strange versus normal.

His eyes paused when he saw a bewildered-looking young boy standing in the field across from him. The boy was dressed in a bright green shirt and bright purple pants. His thick-rimmed black glasses were a little off-kilter and the boy's red hair was a mess.

"Hello?" asked the confused-looking boy.

The kangaroo-duck cocked his head and stared at the boy. He searched his mind for an appropriate response but only a few words jumped out from his bill. "Hola con queso!" he squawked at the boy.

An unnatural desire to be in the city on the horizon gripped the kangaroo-duck at that moment, and he sped away from the brightly attired boy. As the animal hopped toward the strange-looking city at the end of the field, the kangaroo-duck suddenly vanished. His last thoughts were, *Donde está Toonopolis*. Then he ceased to exist.

* * *

Juan Hernandez looked at the ball of paper on the floor. He had just watched his son get bored with the drawing of the kangaroo-duck, crumple the artwork into a ball, and toss it aside. Carlos was already working on a new drawing of a familiar cartoon character that Juan saw on the television regularly.

Juan placed his coffee cup on the table and bent down to retrieve his son's discarded art. Opening up the wrinkled sheet, he pondered the kangaroo-duck. "I guess it's a good thing these drawings don't have feelings, huh?"

"Of course they don't, papi, it's just a drawing."

"I suppose you're right," Juan replied. "But I like this one. Can I keep it?"

Carlos nodded and reached for his yellow crayon again. He began coloring in the square underwater creature on the page. Juan folded the picture of the kangaroo-duck and looked forward to adding it to the growing stack of original Carlos Hernandez drawings that Juan kept in his bedroom.

Juan didn't even realize that he was the only reason these creatures continued to exist in the cartoon city of Toonopolis. Maybe someday he'll find out.

The Legend of the Chucacabra

Author note:

This short story introduced a brand new section of Toonopolis (Westoria) as well as a character who would become important in her own right (Misanthrope Beechworth from Steamport). It also features a few other characters first introduced in *Toonopolis: Gemini* (Yuki from Animetown and Plucky McGee from Supercity!).

It was first published in *Demonic Wildlife*, a dark humor anthology published by Battle Goddess Productions in October 2017 and edited by Valerie Willis.

The Legend of the Chucacabra

We all gathered around the bonfire for one last storytelling session before we left Camp Westoria for home sections of Toonopolis. The experience was one to remember for those of us from areas of our cartoon city that didn't remotely resemble the American Old West like this one. I made great friends hailing from diverse corners of Toonopolis such as Camenot, Pixelburgh, Supercity, and Steamport. My own home, Animetown, was almost as far from Westoria as a section of Toonopolis could be.

After all the horseback riding, story swapping, gun shooting, and trail hiking, we would sit at the bonfire eating our evening meal (tonight it was hamburgers) and listen to a story told by Wayne Northwood, the oldest and most respected guide/cowboy in all Westoria. That last night, Wayne made it clear he saved his most chilling story for last.

"Let me tell yer," Wayne began, instantly silencing the murmurs around the bonfire, "I done saved my most chilling story for last." His weatherworn eyes creased even further into a far-off gaze as he stared through us all and into the darkness behind us. He ran his hand through his white, frontiersman beard in a sagely fashion. His voice was slightly muffled by the wad of chewing tobacco he always kept tucked in his left cheek.

"This is the Legend of the Chucacabra."

He allowed for silent reverie at the title. There were whispers among the campers but the crackling of wood in the bonfire dominated the airwaves.

"Don't you mean Poopacabra?" asked the sarcastic sidekick from Supercity, Plucky McGee.

A death glare from Wayne silenced the snark instantly. Time at Camp Westoria, especially at the shooting range, made everyone at camp respect Wayne's eagle-eyed stare. If he drew on us, nothing we could do would stop him from gunning us down. I was pretty sure he'd never actually do it, but I also was pretty sure I didn't want to find out if he would.

"The Legend of the Chucacabra," he said again through gritted teeth. This time, no one interrupted him and our hushed silence grew even deeper. We settled in and prepared for Wayne's story. The way he told his stories would transport us directly into them, almost as if we were framed inside the story within our own story.

"Some say the Chucacabra haunts Westoria to this day. But it wasn't always a demonically possessed creature of death and destruction, no sir. As the story goes, it was once a regular coyote, prowling the desert hills of Westoria just like any other coyote would do: hunt at night, sleep during the day, and stay away from people. Quite misanthropic, coyotes."

He tossed a grin to Missy, our friend from Steamport whose full name was Misanthrope

The Legend of the Chucacabra

Beechworth. She fidgeted with her goggles nervously. He continued, "One coyote, however, grew bolder. You see, as human settlements encroached into the wilderness more and more, the coyote's habitat shrank more and more. For most of the coyotes, this meant they decreased their range to continue staying away from people. This clever coyote, however, began to embrace the humans and realized that among the wastefulness and destruction of humankind could be found free food.

You see, hunting is hard work cowboys and cowgirls, as you've come to learn in your stay at Camp Westoria. Why buy the horse when you can get the meat for free, after all?"

A sound of disgust went up from the gathered campers, who were either looking at their plates of food, clutching their stomachs, or on the verge of vomiting into the bonfire. I personally felt no problem with the idea that we were eating horsemeat. *Basashi* was not an uncommon dish in Animetown, after all. I guessed the rest of my campmates weren't as keen on the idea. I shrugged and took another bite of my hamburger (or horseburger).

"Oh settle down, you daisies," Wayne spat. "It's just a saying. You're eating cow, not horse."

Several of the campers looked relieved. A few still looked at their plates of food side-eyed and were clearly done eating for the night.

Wayne Northwood smiled his wry smile, suggesting his choice of words was not an accident but simply a gag he liked to play on the campers. I found this easy to believe because the man never said something he didn't mean to say. Even if he did, he made it so easy to feel like it was on purpose that it might have well been.

"You see, campers, before humans moved in on the coyote territory, the coyotes would hunt rabbits, rodents, and even larger game like deer and bison. They'd even go after small birds."

A sound went up from an unidentified camper and Wayne Northwood held up his hand immediately to silence the question he could tell was coming.

"Now afore you all go off on that famous coyote and roadrunner situation, let me stop you. We live in a world of fact, even in the Tooniverse. Some of you may come from some pretty fantastical sections of Toonopolis." He pointed to me and said, "Yuki there comes from a really wacky part without a lot of grounding in reality."

I wasn't sure to take offense or to agree with him. Sure, Animetown seemed perfectly normal if it was all you ever knew, but having travelled to other sections of the Tooniverse, I knew it was pretty far on the absurd end of the spectrum at times. Even so, I felt I should defend my home section so I stuck out my tongue and took my right index finger to my lower right eyelid and pulled it down.

"Don't you *akanbe* me, son," the cowboy said immediately.

I quickly pulled in my tongue and released my eyelid. Not only did he see me through the fire and smoke, he even knew what my expression was called in Japanese. There really wasn't getting anything past this old man. I looked down at my feet.

"And don't none of the rest of you think about eyeballin' me or sassin', ya hear? I thought you all done learned that by now." He cleared his throat. "As I were sayin', in Westoria we are grounded in the grit and reality of life. This here section of Toonopolis is firmly rooted in the American Old West, myself included.

Now in the real world, a roadrunner is no match racing a coyote, even without all them fancy gizmos and gadgets. A roadrunner can only reach a top speed of twenty miles per hour while a coyote can get up to nearly forty-five miles per hour. Of course, roadrunners can fly so they wouldn't try to outrun a coyote in the first place, they'd just fly away. So leave all that nonsense out of your heads.

Now this one coyote decided he was gonna take the easy road and start scavenging off the human civilization moving in around them. Why chase a rabbit or fight with a cobra when the humans would just leave piles of food in containers right next to their buildings? Luckily for this coyote, he never ate anything he wasn't supposed to eat and get hisself sick. Unluckily, though, he got something far worse."

He took a deep breath and paused for effect.

"One day while he was foraging out back of a Generic Offbrand Mexican Restaurant, he stumbled across something that tore apart his insides—"

"Right?" Plucky McGee interrupted. "That stuff really goes through me, too."

A gunshot went off before any of us even saw any movement. The stool where the sidekick from Supercity was sitting collapsed under him and he tumbled to the ground hard. I watched him get to his feet, dust himself off, and look at the stool that was now missing a leg. I followed my eyes back to Wayne Northwood, who was holding his six-shooter. The gun had a thin tendril of smoke coming out of the barrel.

"I done warned you, kid," he said.

"I can't help it!" Plucky responded. "I'm a superhero sidekick. I have to make the sarcastic poop jokes. It's in my nature."

Wayne nodded, "That's why the bullet hit your chair instead of you. Or did you think I missed?"

Plucky shook his head violently. None of us would have thought he missed. Wayne Northwood never missed. Plucky tried to put his stool back together but quickly realized that a two-legged stool that was supposed to have three legs was not very useful as a seat anymore. He sighed and sat in the dirt instead.

Wayne seemed satisfied with Plucky's punishment and continued, "Now when I say insides, I don't mean the coyote's guts." He paused and glared at Plucky, who made a 'mouth zipped' motion with his hand across his lips. "I mean the soul of the coyote. You see: there is a nasty little type of demon that likes to frequent Mexican restaurants called a Caca Demon. This demon likes to hide itself among the heat and spices so you don't taste it.

To humans, a Caca Demon is mostly harmless. Like Mr. McGee said a few moments ago, they contribute to the food 'going right through you' I believe were his words." He looked at Plucky, who nodded. "A Caca Demon only takes a tiny bit of your soul on the way through. This is why people will often feel really bad after a big Mexican fast food meal. Well, that and the flaming diarrhea."

Several people laughed. A few people looked around to see if they were allowed to laugh. It was hard to tell if Wayne was joking or serious because he always was so stern. Of course, he did make jokes from time to time and it seemed he liked to torture us into trying to figure out if laughter was appropriate. It appeared to be okay in this case because none of the laughers got scolded. By the time we sorted it out, though, the moment had passed and the humor was gone. Thus was the beautiful irony of a Wayne Northwood joke.

"As I was sayin'," he said, casting another glare at Plucky, "the Caca Demon is mostly harmless to us. But to a coyote, well, no one ever knew what one would do until it did.

One night, not unlike tonight, a worker at the Generic Offbrand Mexican Restaurant was clearin' out the trash at the end of his shift and heard a rustlin' by the trashcans. The boy assumed it was just a round tailed squirrel or a rabbit, desert critters that would often eat the leftover greens or insects around the trash. What he found there was something else entirely."

Wayne once again paused for dramatic effect. He let his eyes sweep the gathered campers and then spit out of the corner of his mouth and continued. "What that young man found all them years ago was a coyote. But he could tell right away that this was no ordinary coyote. Your average Westoria coyote, as you know, is about three to four feet long with a foot, foot-and-a-half long tail. This creature shared that with the coyote it once was, but that was about it.

Where it once had fur, the animal had dry, scaly looking skin. Its eyes were sunken in and red as a bottle of Tabasco sauce. Its spine and tail were distorted, curved up almost like the four-legged beast was trying to become a two-legged creature. Along the ridges of its spine were four to five-inch-long spikes that looked like they grew right out of the vertebrae. Its lips were nearly non-existent, pulled back to reveal even bigger and sharper fangs than any coyote should possess.

And when this young man realized he was staring at a monster, he did what any good Westoria boy would do."

Wayne took a pause and looked around. It seemed like he was looking for a response from someone but no one spoke up. So I asked, "What was that?"

Wayne removed his gun from its holster with his lightning-quick draw and pointed it at me, "He shot at the bastard with his six-shooter, o' course."

"Did he hit it?" I followed, while moving my head slightly to the side to no longer be in the sights of his gun.

Wayne smiled coyly and slipped his gun back into the holster smoothly. "Yer damn right he did." He punctuated the statement with a spit of his chewing tobacco into the fire. A pungent puff of smoke curled out from where he spat.

"But it didn't do jack or squat to the beast. The former coyote screeched at him and fell back to four legs after a shot hit him squarely in the side. In a regular coyote, it would have been a direct strike to the heart and left him dead instantly. In this creature, a foul-smelling black ooze came from the wound and left a trail of liquid crap like it had dysentery as it fled back into the desert."

"Crap?" Missy asked.

"They might call it night soil where you're from, Missy. Feces, excrement," Wayne paused and looked at Plucky McGee, who looked like he was going to burst from keeping his comments to himself any longer. "Go ahead, Plucky."

"POOOOOOOOOP!" Plucky shouted from his place on the dirt ground.

"I see," Missy replied. "Thank you, sir."

"Why can't you be more proper like her, Plucky?" Wayne asked.

"Because she's from snooty Steamport and I'm from Supercity?" he replied.

"I'll have you know," Missy began once again fiddling with the goggles around her neck, "that being polite and proper knows no bounds, regardless of status or upbringing."

Plucky rolled his eyes. This was a common exchange I'd observed between my two friends over the course of camp. No matter what happened next, neither would budge from their position so they learned to just stop before it turned into an hours-long debate. The rest of us were quite appreciative when they figured this out.

The Legend of the Chucacabra

"So the creature left a trail of *unpi*?" I asked, trying to get the story back on course.

"That it did, Yuki," Wayne replied. "Liquid stool from the trashcans back to the desert. The young man wanted to track the creature and finish the job, but he had to finish wiping down the prep stations in the restaurant and did not want to be derelict to his duties.

After that night, other reports began pouring in around Westoria about the foul creature that once was a coyote. Anyone who was able to land a shot on the beast reported the same reviling ooze in place of blood. And it seemed to heal from the wounds immediately, the ooze plugging the hole and keeping the critter alive, no matter how badly injured.

This is where the creature earned its nickname: Chucacabra. It derived its name from the Chupacabra, a legend of Latin America in the Real World, but you know, with poop inside of it."

Plucky let out a loud guffaw. I was afraid Wayne was going to shoot at him again and, this time there was no stool for him to shoot out instead.

Luckily, Wayne just shrugged and said, "I don't disagree Plucky. But I weren't the one to name it. But the name stuck with the dimwit locals and there you have it. And that, boys and girls, is the Legend of the Chucacabra."

A round of disappointment came from the gathered campers. A few of them even started booing and crying out complaints.

"What do you mean?"

"How is that all?"

"Lame!"

"What happened to it?" I added to the cacophony.

Wayne held up a hand to silence us and it was quite effective. "Now now, kids. One at a time." He pointed to a squire-looking kid from Camenot whose name I forget.

"Sir Wayne," he began.

"I told you before, I ain't no sir," Wayne responded tersely.

"Yes, sorry, sir. Um, I mean, Mr. Wayne. But how is that the entirety of the story? What happened to it?" the squire asked earnestly. I was glad he stole my question so I could stay quiet.

"Nothing," the cowboy said.

"What the hell?" Plucky spat out.

Wayne's eyes flew open wide and he stared at Plucky. "Hell indeed, Mr. McGee. Because some say that's where the demon creature fled to after being hunted by so many ranchers and restaurant owners for trespassing and eating their livestock and trash."

The campers settled back down, realizing Wayne was not really done but was just baiting them.

The Legend of the Chucacabra

"The sheriff rounded a posse of folk willing to head into the desert to track the beast, but they couldn't find him. One day, reports of the Chucacabra just stopped coming in and the fear died down. Some say it finally died of its wounds. Some say it fled to another section of Toonopolis. Still others, myself included, say it returned to the hell from whence the Caca Demon originally came and waits for the perfect moment to return to the surface and feed once again."

The campsite devolved once again to complete silence save the crackling of the bonfire. The campers all looked at each other and around into the darkness of the desert around them. Several of us inched our stools closer to the fire and away from the darkness. The gleam in Wayne Northwood's eye suggested he knew exactly what he was doing with the way he told the story. Plucky raised his hand tentatively.

Wayne made eye contact with him and nodded. "Mr. Northwood, how do we know this story isn't full of as much caca as the coyote?" He asked the question seriously but clearly his word selection wasn't the best. That was Plucky for you.

The cowboy reached into the C-space behind him and pulled out a purple visor. It was really old and worn and the faded yellow letters on the front read "Generic Offbrand Mexican Restaurant" in fancy script. "Because, Mr. McGee," he said while removing his cowboy and placing the visor over his long gray hair, "I was that young worker who was the first to spy the creature and strike the first blow."

The campers gasped, oohing and aahing at the revelation. Plucky was left dumbstruck. I wasn't sure if Wayne was telling the truth or just playing out a longer ruse, but it sure was convincing and we had learned never to be too surprised at the things Wayne has seen and done in his long years. Suffice to say, though, we all had a little trouble sleeping that last night in camp, wondering if every sound we heard in the desert around us might be the Chucacabra, returning from hell to feast once again.

Anchihiiroo – Origin of an Antihero

Author Note:

After *Toonopolis: Gemini* was first published, I was left with a lot of characters that got very little "screen time" in that story. Almost immediately, I began working on this novella to tell the backstory of Anchihiiroo or Han'Eiyuu, the rogue of Animetown that Gemini faced in the first novel. I thought it would be fun to explore the origin story of just how an antihero is born (and understand why Yoshi decided to go rogue in the first place!).

** 23 **

This novella was first published in December 2011 by Portmanteau Press LLC. It was since re-edited by Jessica West. This is the first time this novella is available in print!

Part Zero: The Introduction

I had to force my creator to change me into a villain. Only then did I become what I envisioned myself to be. I never wanted to be a hero. Some would agree that it doesn't make sense that I was hailed as a hero in the first place.

Since a hero is what my creator wanted me to be, that's what I became—against all logic. In other sections of Toonopolis, they referred to somebody like me as an anti-hero—a 'good guy' who doesn't really possess the qualities that most people expect from a hero. In Animetown, I became known as Anchihiiroo. This is my story.

Part One: The Survivor

I don't recall what my parents looked like. I was only about five years old when the great Ninja-Pirate War spreading throughout Toonopolis found its way into the small villages surrounding the heart of Animetown. My hometown, Higeki, was among the first to feel the effects of a war that had nothing to do with us. Our riverside village represented a strategic location to capture for the pirates to gain a foothold into Animetown.

My parents were killed in the onslaught of the pirate invasion. They were simple folk who didn't know how to protect themselves from seasoned warriors like these invaders. It took only a few of the scoundrels to break through the meager defenses of our home.

My mother had me hidden in a small cupboard under the stairs and told me to be silent, no matter what I heard—including the screams of my mother and father as the pirates cut them down. Through the slits in the wooden door, the face of the one who struck the final blows was burned into my memory. The pirate was an older, pale-skinned man with long, yellow hair. His green eyes were rounder than mine and showed no signs of mercy. His mouth drew into a smirk. I held in a scream.

I can't remember my parents' faces, but I never relinquished the image of that man.

After the pirates finished ransacking our house, I snuck out through the back door and ran as fast as my five-year-old legs could carry me. Maybe I should have been frozen in fear by what I'd seen, but a voice in my mind just told me to run. I luckily avoided the pirates during my escape and found my way to the dirt road that connected Higeki to the neighboring seaside village of Hiun.

I think I made it halfway before my little legs gave out and I fell to the side of the road in exhaustion. The internal voice that had told me to run fell asleep a few moments before I did.

* * *

I awoke in a comfortable bed, clean and safe. It took a moment to remember my parents and that terrible pirate's smirking face. I screamed.

"Do not fear, young one," came a calm voice beside my bed.

I turned toward an elderly woman in a red silk kimono. She was old but she was pretty. She had soft, kind eyes that made me think of my grandmother. I looked into those eyes—dark eyes framed with wrinkles—and cried.

The woman took me into a matronly embrace and ran her hands through my shoulder-length, black hair. "It's okay, child. You are safe now." She pushed me slightly away from her so she could look into my face. "You are from Higeki, are you not?"

I simply nodded through my sobs.

"What is your name?"

"Y-y-yoshi," I replied.

"Well, Yoshi—"

"Touji," a deep male voice interrupted the woman, "we have a message regarding Higeki."

I looked over her shoulder at a strong-looking man in fisherman's clothing.

"Quiet, Maebure. The child from Higeki is awake."

The rebuke from the gentle woman seemed to sting the large man, who bowed and backed out of the room.

Touji slowly stood and patted me on the head. "I will be right back, Yoshi."

I waited for Touji to exit the room before slowly sliding out of the bed. I wanted to hear about my village and the large fisherman seemed to have news, so I crept to the door and pressed my ear to a small opening the old woman left.

"...no survivors, Touji," Maebure said.

I could hear the frown in Touji's voice when she responded. "The pirates killed everyone? Surely, some people must have fled?"

"The pirates were ruthless in chasing people down. They were waiting in the river for those who tried to flee on their boats. If anyone else got away, we didn't find them."

"Then the boy is the only survivor from Higeki," Touji said with a sigh.

"So it would seem. I have worse news, though." Maebure looked scared.

It was strange to see a man so grown and so large be scared. It wasn't until later in life that I learned size and age have nothing to do with fear.

Touji guessed the news. "The pirates are not content with Higeki, are they?"

Maebure shook his head. "They are loading up spoils from Higeki and ships are already moving upriver towards Hiun."

The old woman sighed again. "We can only hope that the ninjas come to our defense in time."

"Shouldn't we try to evacuate?"

"If these pirates are as ruthless as you've described, it is useless. We cannot outrun them in our fishing vessels and there is nowhere for us to go if we flee by land."

I must have been listening a little too eagerly to the conversation between the two adults because I lost my footing and fell face-first through the doorway. My body landed in a dust-cloud at their feet. Looking up at the old woman and the fisherman, I tried to give them a cute smile.

It didn't work.

"Yoshi, were you listening to us?" Touji asked in a calm but stern voice. I nodded, tears stinging my eyes.

"Not to be cold in front of the boy, Touji, but what should we do?" Maebure asked.

Touji picked me up off the ground with more ease than I expected from an old lady.

I nestled my face into her neck as she talked to Maebure over my shoulder.

"Take Yoshi to the orphanage and hide the children. We must prepare for the worst and hope the ninjas come to our aid in time."

I pulled my head away from the old woman and glanced at Maebure.

He made to argue with her but I could see that he knew it was pointless. He reached his arms out to me.

I pulled back and hid my face in Touji's shoulder.

"It's okay, Yoshi."

I looked into Touji's eyes.

"Maebure will take you to play with the other children of Hiun. Doesn't that sound like fun?"

Anchihiiroo – Origin of an Antihero

I knew she was just trying to make me feel better and it didn't work at all. But I mumbled in agreement and allowed Maebure to take me into his strong arms.

He held me with one arm as if I were weightless.

It felt very safe to be held by such a strong man after everything I had seen.

We exited Touji's home and entered the tense atmosphere in the village of Hiun. I could tell right away that all of the villagers knew the pirates were on their way. People frantically shuffled their families into their homes and barred their doors.

"Maebure," I began, "will the ninjas save us?"

The large man looked at me and smiled. "Of course they will, Yoshi."

I didn't voice my doubt to him, but I knew his conviction was insincere. A child can sense such things.

We quickly arrived at our destination: a small rectangular building with a soft glow coming from the inside. Maebure slid open the rice-paper door and placed me inside the entrance. A few other children played on the far end of the building. They looked a little older than me.

"Go play, Yoshi. Things will be okay." The doubt in his voice was obvious.

I watched the other kids play as the door closed behind me. The largest of the kids turned his attention to me after Maebure left. He didn't look very friendly. I didn't like the way he was staring at me. I really didn't like it when he smiled at me.

"New kid," he said.

I guessed he was around eight or nine.

"Leave him alone, Ijimekko," one of the other children said.

The big kid snapped his head toward the one who spoke. He moved with such force, I was surprised his head didn't fall off.

The one who'd tried to defend me shrank back against a wall.

Ijimekko looked back at me and I decided I didn't want to be there anymore. I opened the rice-paper door and, for the second time in as many days, I ran. I don't know if the big kid chased me because I never looked back.

I didn't rest until I climbed a large hill that overlooked Hiun. A sakura orchard covered the top of the hill. The cherry blossoms were in full bloom and smelled wonderful. I curled up at the base of one of the trees and tried to become smaller.

* * *

I must have fallen asleep because I woke up and it was nighttime. I simultaneously heard voices whispering next to me and pained screams coming from the village below. The pirates had started their attack on Hiun. I scanned the orchard to find the source of the nearby whispering.

"Kunoichi," a male voice whispered, "we must respond. We cannot let the pirates gain another foothold into our territory."

Two shadowed figures stood out in stark contrast against the moon. The light was low and they wore black clothing. They hated the pirates. They wore black. They carried katanas on their backs. This could only mean one thing: ninjas!

My heart rose. They had come to save us.

Then I heard the icy reply from the other ninja, a woman. "Burn them back to their boats." She paused. "Then burn their boats."

"What about Hiun's villagers?"

"Probably already dead or close to it by now. Burn the village to the ground. All of you need practice on your Katon Jutsu anyway."

"Kuno—"

"You have your orders, Naito," the female ninja snapped. "We are not here to win popularity contests. We are trying to win a war and I have received word that Boreas is among the pirates. If we can kill their king, they will have no order. We have a chance to end this war tonight. If a few lives are lost along the way, so be it. Now go."

I couldn't believe what I heard the ninja lady saying. I thought the ninjas were coming to protect

Hiun, but all she cared about was ending the war and killing the pirate king.

I curled into a smaller ball at the base of the tree but kept my eyes on the two figures. The male ninja, Naito, bowed to Kunoichi then swiftly retreated.

Kunoichi stood alone, her figure still outlined by the moon behind her. She sighed and turned her attention directly to me.

"I am sorry, child, but you observed too much," she said with only a hint of actual apology in her tone. I saw the rapid motion of her hands before the large fireball hurtled towards my tree.

With the added light of the fireball, I could see the exposed portion of her face. Her skin was the same color as mine but it was her rare green eyes that stood out, jade gems that would never escape my memory. I closed my own eyes and braced for the flames.

Part Two: The Prophecy

I awoke choking on water. This really confused me because the last memory I had before shutting my eyes was of a giant fireball heading toward me from the hands of a female ninja. I had no idea where the water came from but didn't have too much time to think because I was actively drowning.

I opened my eyes to try to figure out where I was—aside from underwater. Charred remains of the beautiful sakura trees surrounded me. I was still in the grove. The water had come to me.

I tried to kick my legs to break the surface, but they wouldn't move. They were pinned under a fallen tree.

Panicking is the worst thing you can do when you're holding your breath. I learned that later, in training, but it would have been useful to my five-year-old self, who became frantic and used up the last of his oxygen in seconds.

I looked up at the surface and saw a small boat cutting a line in the water. A hand reached down and grabbed me by the collar. In seconds, I was freed and spitting out water on the bottom of the boat. A few bald men looked down at me, then my eyes rolled back into my head.

A strong sense of *déjà-vu* overwhelmed me when I awoke again. I was beginning to think my life was becoming a repetition of barely escaping death and waking shortly thereafter in a warm bed. The cycle had repeated itself as I woke up clean, dry, and apparently unharmed.

I gazed at my surroundings. An old Buddhist monk was sweeping the wooden floor by my bedside. His head was shaved and he wore an orange robe over a longer, white robe. He must have felt my gaze because he stopped sweeping to smile down at me.

"What happened?" I asked.

"What do you recall?"

"I saw the ninjas. I thought they came to save us. She told them to burn the village to get the pirates. Then she tried to kill me." I was nearly in tears by the end.

The monk sat on the bed next to me and gently placed his hand on my shoulder. He smelled of stinky tofu.

"Where did the water come from?" I asked.

"We were unsure until just now, young one. We thought the fire was from the pirates and the flooding from a destroyed dam."

"The fire was the ninjas. I swear."

"I believe you, child. You have no reason to lie." He sighed. "It would seem the water was also ninjitsu."

"Ninjitsu?" I interrupted.

"Ninja magic. They must have destroyed the dam upstream to make it seem like the pirates did it. So much innocent life has been wasted in this petty war." The last line was mumbled and didn't seem like it was directed at me.

"Where am I now?"

The monk stared off into the distance for a moment.

I didn't think he heard me, but I waited patiently. I sat up. My legs hurt when I shifted them. I had forgotten about the fallen tree that pinned my legs while underwater.

"Suzaku Temple in the main section of Animetown. I am Bikkhu Soohei. We sought survivors in Higeki and Hiun after hearing word of the pirate attacks. We only found one."

I shook my head. I didn't have any tears left after all of the disasters from the last few days. I felt sad for Touji and Maebure, the kind people from Hiun who briefly looked after me. At this point, I had already become numb to death and dying. It wasn't exactly a comfortable thought for a five-year-old to have.

Soohei seemed to sense my feelings. "You are safe now. Even if the ninjas did a horrible thing, they also pushed the pirates away from Animetown. They will not come any closer."

"I guess," I replied.

Soohei jumped to his feet.

I remember being surprised at how limber he was for an old man. "Come, Yoshi, let me show you around your new home." He smiled at me.

"How did you know my name?"

"You spoke in your sleep," he answered.

"Oh." I gingerly swung my legs to the side of the bed.

Soohei retrieved a wheeled chair and brought it to me. He gently placed me into the seat, his smile never wavering.

"Are you ready for the tour?"

His positive energy was infectious and I felt soothed just being in his presence, despite all of the bad things I had witnessed. He pushed me around the temple and showed me all the different sections of my new home. I saw the gardens where they grew their own soybeans and other vegetables. He showed me the sleeping quarters of the trainee monks that he called *samaneras*. Some looked barely older than me.

I was more impressed with the training area where the monks learned *aikido*; a form of fighting that relied mostly on self-defense without injuring your attacker.

"Why *not* hurt someone who wants to hurt you?" I asked.

"Why continue a cycle of pain when you can end it?"

I thought about his question but couldn't come up with a good reason other than my feelings that if I had a chance to inflict pain on those who hurt me so much, I wouldn't hesitate to take it. I kept that thought to myself.

We stopped at a thick wooden door with a red bird painted on the outside.

"What is this room?"

"This is the room that lends our temple its name. Suzaku is housed in here."

"What's a suzaku?"

"Not *a* suzaku. Suzaku. She is a legendary bird, a phoenix. But she currently slumbers."

"So there's a big red bird sleeping behind the door?" I asked.

Soohei laughed. He opened the door and let me look inside. There were wall sconces placed around the room. A fairly large egg sat in a pile of ashes and hay in the center of the room. The egg was probably two feet wide and streaked with red and gold that glittered in the flickering light.

"It's a big egg."

"Yes. And Suzaku sleeps inside. She has been sleeping for over one hundred years. One purpose of our temple is to await the one who will fulfill the prophecy of Suzaku Temple."

"What's a prophecy?"

"It is a series of events that we expect to happen based on stories from long ago. When Suzaku came here to die, she told the monks that she would not awaken again until she was approached by a hero worthy of her companionship."

"Die? But it's an egg."

"Yes. The phoenix dies in a ball of flame. From her ashes arises an egg with a young phoenix inside. She is both the same phoenix as well as her child."

"She's her own mother?" I concluded.

Soohei laughed at my childish perspective. "I suppose you could say that. You see the ash spread across the floor?" he said, pointing.

"Yes."

"It is hot to the touch for anyone who Suzaku does not feel is worthy. When our novice monks turn thirteen, we test each one of them to see if they are the ones to fulfill the prophecy. So far, all we have seen are burned feet." He laughed quietly at his joke. Soohei gently closed the door to Suzaku's room.

"What else do people learn here?" My mind returned to the monks practicing martial arts.

Soohei rubbed his chin. "I suppose I can show you. You've never been exposed to other parts of Toonopolis before, but you know that Animetown is just a small part of a larger world, right?"

"Yes."

He guided me down a corridor and opened another door. Inside, I watched some of the older monks doing very strange things. I saw one monk pull a large club out from behind his back. It seemed to come from nowhere. Another was walking on air until he looked down and fell into a heap.

"What is this?" I asked.

"There are laws governing our world that we in Animetown are still learning about. Other parts of Toonopolis seem to accept them as normal but we have been exploring them as well. It is quite like–"

"Magic," I finished.

"Not entirely. It is more like–"

"Not interested." My curt answer seemed to set Bikkhu back a moment. After hearing about ninjitsu, I had no desire to learn anything else about the magic of Animetown or any other parts of Toonopolis.

"Come," Soohei said, breaking my thoughts. "I want you to meet another young boy who recently arrived here."

I stared at the red bird on the door until Soohei wheeled me away. He took me to a small room littered with metal parts, screws, and other debris. A strange-looking boy lifted his head as we approached, and smiled. He wore loose-fitting goggles and a smaller version of the robes that the rest of the Suzaku Temple monks wore.

His hair and skin were pure white. He was probably a few years older than me, but we were the same size.

"Greetings, Bikkhu Soohei," he said jovially. His hands were busy using a screwdriver to either put together or take apart—I couldn't tell which—a small mechanical device.

"Yuki recently came here from a family in Animetown, Yoshi."

My five-year-old mind didn't filter the next question. "Why is he so white?"

Yuki lifted his goggles to reveal a pair of pale blue eyes. His good nature didn't falter. "I am an albino. There is nothing wrong with me, so don't worry, Yoshi. I just don't have color in my skin, unlike you."

He placed his tools down and walked to me. He put out his hand and I shook it.

Soohei seemed pleased. "I will leave you two to get to know each other. Since you are the two newest residents here, I hope that you will become friends."

The Bikkhu left us.

Anchihiiroo – Origin of an Antihero

Yuki offered to show me the mechanical devices he was working on. It was so interesting and Yuki loved to talk about them.

Soohei probably knew Yuki would be a good distraction, but I didn't have time to think about the old monk's intentions. Yuki kept my mind racing with his talk of robotics and gears and wheels.

Thus my time at Suzaku Temple began. I was treated no differently than any of the other novice monks. When I turned seven, I received my own set of robes and began my training in the Order of Suzaku.

* * *

The next five years passed with little to note. My training taught me the Buddhist principles of mindfulness and peace. I learned how to cultivate vegetables and to prepare them. I was trained in *aikido*. The monks also allowed younger novices like Yuki and I time to play and be children.

Yuki's thirteenth birthday came and went and he only got burnt feet for his attempt at approaching Suzaku's egg. I was only a few months away from my thirteenth birthday, as best as the monks could guess. No one knew the actual date of my birth.

Yuki wasn't surprised that he wasn't the hero of the prophecy. His genius with robotics continued to grow and he was working with a crazy idea that he could build some sort of artificial intelligence and make one of his machines come to life. He spent much more time in his tinkering room than anywhere else.

Even though he was two years older than me, I far surpassed his size and ability in physical activities by the time I was ten. We grew to be as close as brothers over the years, our differences being the glue that brought us together.

Some of the kids were playing hide and seek one day when I broke one of the major rules of Suzaku Temple. There was a small spot in Suzaku's egg room just on the other side of the door that had no ash on the floor. I figured that would be an amazing hiding spot.

I ran to the wooden door with the red bird on it and snuck quietly inside. I pulled the door shut and stood on my toes to keep my heels from touching the ash on the floor. I could hear kids outside being found and the seeker running past the door.

My legs began to cramp. Finally, the other kids called for me. "Yoshi! You win, Yoshi! You can come out!"

I breathed a sigh of relief. Then the flames on the wall sconces shot up in the air and caught me completely off guard. I spun in place and lost my footing, falling into the ash on Suzaku's floor.

My screams alerted the other kids to my location. Yuki was the one to open the door. I looked up from the floor and realized that I wasn't feeling any pain. Yuki looked stunned and told one of the other kids to get Bikkhu Soohei.

"Yoshi? Are you okay?" he asked.

I stood up and looked at the wall sconces. They were flickering in their normal state again. I wondered if the flame bursts were just my imagination. I was covered in the phoenix's ashes but wasn't burning. A realization hit me when Soohei came to the door. I barely heard Yuki's question.

"Yoshi! Are you burnt? What happened?" Soohei's voice had more concern than anger, but I could tell he wasn't pleased with me for being in the room before I was thirteen.

I brushed the ash off my robes and gave a thumbs-up. "I am okay, Bikkhu. I am not burnt."

A giant crackling sound behind me diverted attention away from me. I turned and watched as a large fissure appeared in Suzaku's egg.

"It is you," Soohei said. "You are the one of the prophecy, Yoshi."

"I'm what?"

All the children raised in Suzaku Temple had some hope that they would be the one to awaken the legendary bird on their thirteenth birthday. None of us really expected it, however.

"Suzaku?" I asked the cracking egg.

The fissure opened wider and a flare of motion arose from the egg. Suzaku was absolutely beautiful.

No description of the phoenix could have matched what I witnessed that day. She arose without any of the normal wet, sticky goo that I had seen covering hatchling chickens and ducks.

She spread her wings and her red and orange feathers glinted in the light of the fires on the wall. Her tail feathers reached almost to the floor even though she was hovering about five feet in the air. Her wingspan was around three feet and her body was approximately the size of a large hawk's. She stared right at me and spoke with the voice a young girl, high and pleasant.

"You have finally come to me, hero."

"I have?"

"I have slept in that egg for over one hundred years," she said with a bite in her voice. "Please don't tell me I woke up for an idiot."

Her sharp tone caught me off guard. The insult she threw didn't really mesh with how beautiful she was. She flew down and landed at my feet, kicking up some of her ash.

"Cat got your tongue, kiddo?" she asked. "You know who I am, right?"

"Suzaku. This temple was built around you to keep your egg safe while awaiting the hero of your prophecy to awaken you."

She flew into the air again and looked over my shoulder, "Good, Soohei, at least you educated him properly. I thought I was going to have to die again."

"You know me, Miss Suzaku?" Soohei asked. I had never seen him at a loss before.

"I'm a light sleeper," she said with a chuckle.

I made eye contact with her and her eyes seemed to change color in the flickering firelight. "You're not what I expected," I blurted.

"Yeah, neither are you, so let's just get the disappointment out of the way." She hovered in the air again and looked me over. "I feel in you a great destiny, though, which is why I awoke and why my ash did not burn you. You are to be great, Yoshi, and I am here to help you."

I could hear Soohei and the novices gasp behind me. I felt a swell of pride. The phoenix had chosen me. I looked at the Bikkhu and my friends. Some of the other kids looked jealous. A few seemed a little annoyed. Only Yuki and Soohei beamed with pride to match my own.

I exited the room with Suzaku flying over me. The crowd backed up and formed a circle around the phoenix and me. Soohei approached.

"It's time to start your training, then, Yoshi."

"But I've been training, Bikkhu."

"No. You have been trained as a regular monk, my son. You must be trained to be a warrior now. You must become strong in mind, body, and spirit. You must seek out the three greatest senseis in Animetown and learn from them before you are ready to become the great hero you are destined to be."

"But first," said Suzaku, "I have to pee." As everyone stared at her, she responded, "What? You try living in an egg for a hundred years and see if you don't have to pee when you get out."

She gracefully flew past the novices and through an open window in the hall. All eyes turned back to me. I shrugged. "At least she went outside?" I offered as a justification.

"Yoshi, let's get you prepared for your journey," said Soohei.

Suzaku flew back into the hall and landed next to me. She looked at the novices gathered around. "I feel much better; thanks for asking." We followed Bikkhu Soohei down the hall to prepare me for my hero journey.

Part Three: The Mind Sensei

"**I**'m hungry," Suzaku declared as we stood outside the entrance of the Buddhist temple a few months after she hatched.

"You've been eating non-stop for the past two months," I replied. "Are you fattening up for a holiday?"

"*Hrmph*." She nipped my ear.

"*Ow!*"

"That'll teach you to call a lady fat. I'm a growing bird. I need to eat."

I wanted to respond that she wasn't much of a lady, but I figured it was best to just leave well enough alone. Soohei and Yuki observed the exchange from nearby but didn't intervene.

The months after Suzaku's hatching were busy with preparations. Bikkhu Soohei packed my bag with food and water. Suzaku insisted that I gather her ashes from the egg room and carry them on the journey. She said I would need them later but wouldn't tell me why. I packed a few changes of robes but left with nothing else.

I hugged Yuki and said, "You've been like a brother to me. Thank you."

** 49 **

Yuki glanced at Soohei, who nodded. "Funny you should say that—"

"Are we ready to go?" Suzaku interrupted. "We have a lot of traveling to do and this sappy goodbye is upsetting my stomach."

"Are you sure it wasn't the three helpings of breakfast that upset your stomach?" asked Yuki.

Suzaku stuck out her black tongue at Yuki in response.

I laughed, earning myself another nip on the ear from my new friend.

"Yoshi," the Bikkhu began, "do you remember where you need to go to meet your first sensei?"

"To the hills near Hiun. Where the orchard once stood."

"Yes, there is a small hut belonging to a very wise old monk who once resided here but now lives in solitude. He will train your mind to be that of a warrior."

"So you've told me," I responded. "But I still don't understand why I have to train my mind if I am to become a warrior. I need to get stronger."

Soohei laughed.

Suzaku sighed and smacked the back of my head with a wing. "And that's why you need to get smarter first, idiot, because you don't even understand why you need to be able to think to be a hero."

"You're not a very nice bird," I replied while rubbing the spot where she'd slapped me.

"I never said I was."

"Good point."

I walked down the steps to the base of the temple. I turned back to see Soohei and Yuki returning to their lives inside Suzaku's temple. The young phoenix landed on the dirt road next to me and looked up.

"Guess it's just you and me now, kid," she said.

"I guess so," I said, slinging my pack over my shoulder. "Let's go visit the first sensei so I can move on to my real training."

I caught a scoff from Suzaku as she took to the air to follow me away from the temple in the heart of Animetown. It would be years before I would set foot inside Animetown again, although I wasn't aware of that at the time.

* * *

I stood at the base of a familiar hill, looking up at the small, thatched-roof cottage that now rested on top. Years before, I expected to die on that hill as Kunoichi hurled a fireball at me before her ninjas burned Hiun to the ground. My ears grew hot at the memory.

"You gonna eat that?" asked Suzaku, breaking my memories.

"Huh?" I replied before glancing down at the soy-filled bun in my hands. I hadn't eaten any but suddenly didn't feel the urge. I tossed it to the phoenix, who always needed to eat.

"Whadyathikinbout?" she garbled at me with a full mouth.

"Nothing," I replied. The anger dropped from a boil to a simmer as I repacked my bag and began to walk up the hill. It had been a simple two-day walk from Animetown to the monk's hut.

I was quiet as Suzaku observed the remnants of the destruction left from the fire and flood that wiped out Hiun, leaving me as the only survivor. No one had even attempted to rebuild the town. A few half-sunken boats rotted in the small harbor of the former fishing town that took me in after pirates razed my village, Higeki.

I noticed during our trip that Suzaku only seemed to stop talking when she was eating and even then she sometimes tried to do both. She was delighted to add meat to her diet by hunting the large rats that had taken up residence in Hiun. I was raised vegetarian by the monks so wasn't able to help her with that part.

"Waidup!" she cried, gulping down the last of the bun. Her wings loudly beat the air as she rose to fly after me. "Why are you in such a rush, hero?"

"I need to finish my mind training so I can move on to my body training, right?"

"Yeah," she answered, "but if you don't focus on your mind training, you will never make it to the next step."

I groaned. I knew she was right but I had learned very quickly that admitting that to Suzaku usually ended in getting mocked. She insulted me frequently anyway so I tried to avoid giving her more reasons to do so.

As I approached the door to the mind sensei's hut, I noticed a piece of paper pinned to it. It was a note addressed to me.

"Is he not home?" Suzaku asked over my shoulder.

"Yoshi," I read aloud, "before I can train you, you must solve a simple riddle. A man needs to cross a river with a fox, a goose, and some corn. He cannot leave the fox with the goose or the goose with the corn and can only fit one at a time on his boat. How does he cross without losing any of them?"

I glanced at Suzaku, who let out a shrill laugh. "It's an old riddle," she explained.

I continued to read, "Do not knock on my door until you have an answer. If you give me a wrong answer even once, I will not train you. Signed, Bodhi."

I sat down and leaned my back against the hut. I was never good at games like this with the other children. Yuki would usually sort out the answers well before the others. I cheated from him whenever I could. I looked at Suzaku, who was grinning.

"Shut up," I said.

She feigned a hurt look and flew to the top of the hut to perch. I tried to work out the riddle in my head. I kept getting muddled, so I tried talking it out loud instead.

"If he takes the corn first, then—no, the fox would eat the goose. So he has to take the fox or the goose first."

"Should I take a nap?" asked Suzaku from above me.

"You could just tell me the answer and we can be done with this."

"I can't do your homework for you, young man, or you'll never learn," she said in her best motherly voice.

I waved her off and thought about the riddle again. "So he takes the fox first—wait, the goose would eat the corn. Okay, so he has to take the goose first. Then the fox. But the fox would eat the goose on the other side." I smacked myself in the face.

"Did that help?" the phoenix mocked.

"No."

"Try it again, then."

I looked up at her and she covered her face with a wing and pretended to fall asleep. Her fake snoring didn't help me concentrate.

"So if he takes the corn second, the goose would eat the corn if he left it there to go back to the fox."

Suzaku snorted.

I couldn't tell if she was making fun of me or trying to point out a flaw in my logic. I crossed my legs and tried meditating and thinking only on the riddle, ignoring the unhelpful phoenix that was supposed to be my companion.

The answer became clear to me when I stopped worrying about figuring out the answer.

"Ah!" I shouted, rousing Suzaku from her fake sleep. "He must bring the goose first, then on his second trip across, he carries the fox over and brings the goose back after dropping off the fox, switches the goose for the corn, then goes back again for the goose!"

I banged on the door. It opened; a small, ancient man stood inside.

"Took you long enough," he said without humor.

"You were listening to me?"

"Yes. And if you don't speed up your logic, you're going to be here for a very long time. That riddle is for children."

"But I am a child," I answered.

"Then you are no great hero, child. You must remove that idea from your mind. Heroics know no age and a hero is separate from time itself. You must think of yourself as a hero and not a child. We must open your mind, Yoshi."

Suzaku chimed in from the roof. "Maybe you should hit him with a brick then. It will be faster."

"Lady Suzaku," said the old monk, "it is a pleasure to meet you." He bowed, which was awkward since she was on the roof right above him. "You must be hungry after your long sleep. Won't you come in for a meal?"

The phoenix flew down and through a nearby window, landing on a table inside the small hut. She pointed a wing at Bodhi. "See, there's a man who knows how to treat a lady. Let's eat, pops."

"So what do I need to do to finish my mind training?" I asked Bodhi as he prepared food for Suzaku.

"Begin it, for one."

"Wasn't the riddle on the door the beginning?"

Bodhi laughed. "No, that was just to see if you were too dense to teach. That riddle is a basic riddle that most six-year-olds can solve."

My cheeks flushed.

I'm sure Suzaku would have mocked me but her beak was already full of food.

"The first lesson I can give you, Yoshi, is that you must always consider different ways of solving any puzzle set before you."

"Why is this important for me to become a great hero? I should be learning how to fight, to use a sword, to get stronger. How else will I avenge my family?"

Bodhi paused and looked up.

Suzaku stopped eating momentarily to glare at me.

The old monk put a fresh plate of food in front of the phoenix and walked to me.

I was only ten but he had to look up to stare into my face.

"You must put revenge from your mind. You cannot think logically if revenge is your goal. Your destiny is greater than one of revenge. You are to become a hero for all of Animetown, not just for your own vengeance."

He paused and took a deep breath.

"Can you promise me that you are capable of that?"

I looked at Suzaku, who gulped down a mouthful of food and pleaded with her eyes. It was the first time I sensed any sincerity out of her since she hatched, so I looked back at Bodhi and lied.

"Yes, sensei."

The next few months were mundane and repetitive. Bodhi would give me riddles, word puzzles, and number games to work on every day. He had me read histories of Animetown then quizzed me on tiny details.

Before I knew it, nearly a year had passed. I felt like my brain was getting a workout every day. I didn't feel any smarter but I could definitely sense that my thought process had changed over the months. I saw subtle hints in the way sentences were worded in the riddles Bodhi would give me.

Suzaku actually seemed shocked when I would answer a riddle immediately or solve a clever word game before Bodhi even finished telling it. I was finally able to look at puzzles and see answers instead of questions.

Bodhi gave me different riddles. I got stuck on one that he gave me that had a ton of small details and I couldn't figure out how they all pieced together.

"Have you ever heard the phrase, 'not see the forest for the trees'?" Bodhi asked me one day.

"No, what does it mean?"

"That some people get so focused on the trees," Suzaku chimed in, "that they can't see the forest. Sometimes it isn't the details that are important but the whole picture. Sometimes details are useless."

I grinned at my phoenix companion. As I worked on my mind games with Bodhi, she was nicer to me. She had also nearly doubled in size since she hatched. Her six-foot wingspan forced her to stay outside most of the time.

"I understand."

"Good," Bodhi answered, "because I want to give you your final test, the Great Mental Trial."

I perked up. I knew that once I finished with Bodhi, I'd be able to move on to the sensei who would train me on fighting and weapons. I looked at Suzaku, whose head was resting on the windowsill from outside the hut. She nodded at me.

"I'm ready," I said. "Is it a riddle? A puzzle? What?"

Bodhi walked to a nearby cabinet and pulled out a wrapped package. He returned to where I was sitting and placed it on the table. He opened it slowly and revealed a small, multi-colored cube. There were nine spaces on each side of the cube covered with six different colors.

"What is this?"

"The greatest test of the mind, patience, and logic known to man: the Color Cube."

I stole a glance at Suzaku, who nodded in agreement with Bodhi.

"It looks like a toy," I blurted.

"And it is," Bodhi responded. "Sometimes toys and games are the greatest gauge of our abilities. Not everything has to be life and death to test us."

I picked up the cube and rotated the sides. Each of the sides could spin in several directions, moving the colors from one face to another. Bodhi explained that the goal was to make each of the six faces match colors simultaneously.

"That doesn't sound so hard," I replied.

Bodhi laughed. "Then I shall leave you to it. I have an errand to run. I shall be back in the evening."

I rotated the various sides in different directions without thinking. One of the lessons I had learned in the year spent with Bodhi had been that if you over-think things, you might miss how simple they are. This lesson did not help with the cube.

I tried thinking ahead as though I were playing one of Bodhi's number games. I thought about where different colors would end up based on how I rotated. I was able to get one side finished but the other five would be a jumble of colors.

Suzaku watched me for a while before she fell asleep with her head on the windowsill. She had built a nest outside the window so she could participate in the lessons when she wasn't out hunting to sustain her fast-growing size.

"Thanks for your help," I grumbled at my sleeping phoenix friend.

My fingers grew sore, but I finally got three of the sides completed at the same time. I thought about all the lessons Bodhi had given me on logic and how to see the solutions to every puzzle. I also thought about how this little cube was the only thing stopping me from leaving this hut and learning how to be a real warrior.

"I hate this cube!" I screamed and flung the toy at the wall next to Suzaku's window.

The crash woke the giant red bird, who looked at the scattered pieces of the plastic toy and shrugged. "Did that help?"

I walked to the window and looked at the pieces of the Color Cube. I smiled and patted Suzaku on the head. "Yes, it did."

I picked up the half-broken cube and the small squares that came off. I threw the pieces onto the table, ignoring Suzaku's sleepy pleas for an explanation. I rummaged through drawers in Bodhi's hut until I found a jar of adhesive. Back at the table, I broke apart the remaining squares and reassembled the color cube with all six sides matching.

"You seriously just did that?" Suzaku asked.

"What did you say about the forest and the trees?" I reminded her. "The details are useless. I was told the goal was to make the sides match. Do they match?" I held up the completed cube to her.

"I suppose they do, but–"

"But nothing! What did I learn this past year? There are many ways to solve a puzzle. I solved it."

"By throwing it against the wall?"

"Yes."

Suzaku snorted. "You going to explain to Bodhi how you solved it?" My silence answered her question. "Yeah, I didn't think so."

When Bodhi returned from his errand, he praised me for completing the Great Mental Trial so quickly. He gave me the location of the sensei who would train my body for life as a hero. I left the hut with Suzaku following close behind. I hoped the glue would hold long enough for me to get away without getting caught at cheating.

Part Four: The Body Sensei

Suzaku berated me for my deception of Bodhi while we traveled on a small boat from Hiun to the isolated mountain town of Kajiba, home of the next sensei. I tried to remind her that Bodhi never told me I had to follow the rules of the toy to achieve the goal.

The smells of sulfur and fire wafted downriver from the town before we even reached it. When we landed on shore, we noticed that the men and women all had hard features and blackened faces. The people seemed to be carved of stone, like the mountain itself.

Their homes were actually cut into the mountain's face. There were sculpted ladders running up and down the rock for traveling up and down. I could sense immediately that you had to be tough to live here. I was excited to meet the next sensei.

"You must be Yoshi," said a woman who approached me at the shore. She had very short black hair and the same chiseled face and body as all the other residents of Kajiba. She wore a sleeveless shirt and shorts.

"Yes. You know of me?" I beamed.

She pointed to Suzaku, the giant red bird on the ground at my side. "Not too many young men known to be traveling with a phoenix these days."

I felt my cheeks get hot. I had forgotten that Suzaku was much more conspicuous than I was.

"Yeah, don't worry. He may have passed through mind training but he's still kind of an idiot," Suzaku explained.

I ignored Suzaku's insult. "I am here to meet with Tsuyoi for warrior training," I said in my toughest possible voice. "Where can I find him?"

The woman grinned. "You won't find *him* anywhere."

There was a glint in her eye that made me think about how she phrased her response. Maybe Bodhi's teachings weren't all that useless after all?

"You're Tsuyoi, aren't you?"

She directed her response to Suzaku. "I thought you said he was an idiot."

Suzaku shrugged. "Even a dim light bulb gets a spark once in a while."

"So I'm going to learn how to fight from a girl?" I said. It was not a good thing to say. Tsuyoi swept my legs and I landed hard on my back. I looked up and saw Suzaku and Tsuyoi laughing at me. It dawned on me right away that I was going to have to redefine my idea of girls and fighting. I guess the dim light bulb can spark more than once.

Tsuyoi offered me her hand. I was amazed at how strong she was as she effortlessly lifted me to my feet.

"If you ever say anything like that again, your training ends immediately." I could tell she wasn't joking. "You must never underestimate an opponent, whether it be due to size, age, gender, or any other reason."

"Yes, sensei."

Tsuyoi motioned for me to follow her. Suzaku lingered behind. I tilted my head in question at her. "You just got owned," she said.

"Thanks for the update."

Woman or not, Tsuyoi was everything I had hoped for in a sensei. She taught me more offensive maneuvering than the *aikido* taught at Suzaku Temple. When I wasn't training, I was put to work in the forges of Kajiba. I learned that the village's main form of commerce was creating weapons from the minerals mined from the Kajiba Mountain that gave the town its name.

Half a year passed quickly and I loved my time training with Tsuyoi. My body grew stronger. At first, I would become winded after an hour of hard battle training with her. She taught me to push past the exhaustion and keep fighting, finding energy reserves I didn't know I had.

I woke before dawn and started the fires of the forge. After breakfast, I'd train for hours.

Tsuyoi didn't believe in using training weapons and immediately started with real swords. She was so fast and strong and never let me rest. Many nights, I nursed wounds as my new lessons for the day.

That was the routine until I met Gisei.

Being raised in a monastery, I didn't have a lot of experience with girls. The first time I saw Gisei, I nearly burnt down one of the forges. I was operating the foot bellows for the *tatara* of one of the weaponsmiths. I was supposed to maintain the same rhythm to keep the fire at a certain temperature for the steel the smith was forging.

Gisei entered with a basket of bread for the smith, who happened to be her father. I saw her smooth face below her wild, two-toned, spiky hair. I followed the line of her neck with my eyes and did not realize that I had increased the rhythm of the bellows with the increased beating of my heart.

"Yoshi, you idiot!" I heard Suzaku scream from her perch in the rafters of the forge. I had added so much pressure to the forge that the fires spat out of the opening and onto a wooden table nearby. Suzaku flew down and smothered them with her enormous wings.

The story got to Tsuyoi fairly quickly and my lesson that afternoon included a verbal assault about losing focus and some other stuff that I don't remember. Something about Gisei taking my focus away. Tsuyoi ended the lesson quickly.

* * *

I woke up the next morning with a raging headache. It couldn't remember why I was in such pain. Suzaku reminded me.

"Tsuyoi ended your lesson by knocking you unconscious with a kick to the back of your head."

"Ahh," I groaned.

"Yeah, exactly. You need to get up, though, and get to work at the forge."

"I can't focus. I can only think about that girl. Chichi had talked about his daughter before but I can't believe how beautiful she is. She's so . . . wild."

Suzaku flew from the window into the room and landed at the foot of my bed.

"You travel with a giant talking bird and that *girl* strikes you as wild?"

I shook my head. I felt my brain moving around. "You know what I mean, Suzaku. My whole life has always been so controlled since I ended up at the temple at age five. She seems so . . . uncontrolled."

"You got all that from one look at her?"

I swallowed. I didn't want to admit to Suzaku that it was more than just Gisei's wildness that caught my attention.

"Look, Yoshi, you're almost thirteen years old. It's very common for a human boy to start noticing girls, but you don't have the luxury of being a normal boy, if you haven't figured that out by now."

"Says who?"

"Says your destiny. Says me. I slept for a hundred years, waiting to sense the core of a hero for Animetown, Yoshi. I did not hatch to have you throw away your destiny for hormones."

"It's more than that, Suzaku!"

"Sure it is." She shook her head. "You're just a kid–"

"And you're just a stupid bird. What do you know?"

The phoenix opened her beak to speak again but paused. She shook her head. "Fine, then. I'm not going to argue with you about this. Come talk to me when you're ready to be a hero instead of an idiot boy." She flapped her wings in a great gust and tore through the window.

I stared after her momentarily but my thoughts quickly returned to Gisei. I was hoping to catch another glimpse of her that day at the forge but was sent to a different part of Kajiba for work. I mindlessly helped move completed swords and arrowheads into boxes for shipment down the river to other parts of Animetown.

Anchihiiroo – Origin of an Antihero

At lunch that day, I found a small note written in pretty handwriting with my food. Gisei told me to meet her at the riverside this evening. My heart beat at a pace that was unmatched by anything, even my most strenuous battles with Tsuyoi.

I quickly ate my lunch and was at the training grounds before my sensei arrived. She was impressed. "You've never arrived for training before me, Yoshi."

"I learned my lesson from yesterday, sensei." Truthfully, I just didn't want to get knocked unconscious again and miss my meeting with Gisei that night. She took my attentiveness as a sign of renewed focus and it was—just not for the reason she thought. I had one of my finest sessions with my sensei that afternoon and I wasn't even paying attention most of the time. My thoughts were on Gisei.

* * *

I had no trouble sneaking out of my bedroom because I had not seen Suzaku since our fight that morning. Gisei sat by the river, making swirls in the water with her feet. She was beautiful in the moonlight. I could tell she was thinking hard about something by the way she bit her lower lip.

"I got your note," I said quietly.

She jumped up and straightened her dress unnecessarily.

"Yoshi." She bowed her head.

"Yes?"

"I'm glad you came," she mumbled. She looked up at me. Her eyes were calm and beautiful. Her hair, black and streaked with yellow, was as wild as I remembered from the first time I saw her.

"I wouldn't miss it. I actually think I fought better today because I was trying not to let Tsuyoi knock me unconscious again!" I laughed.

She smiled at me and my stomach felt like it did a back flip. Then her smile faded.

"What's wrong?" I asked.

"You're cute," she said.

I scratched my head. I wasn't very experienced with girls, but I thought that being cute was a good thing. Maybe I was wrong.

She laughed at me. That didn't help.

"I have to tell you something," she finally said. "Our meeting wasn't an accident."

I rolled my eyes. "I've heard so much about destiny and fate—sometimes it feels like I don't have control over my own life."

She looked down again and sat back at the river. She patted the ground beside her. I sat next to her, completely baffled by her actions. I'd heard men talk about how hard it was to understand their wives and was starting to suspect that they weren't just complaining without reason.

"This isn't about destiny or fate, Yoshi. I am supposed to tempt you. Tsuyoi instructed me to do so."

"What?"

"Since you are training your body, she wanted to test not just your physical strength but your ability to control your body's desires. She said that a true warrior must have control over all parts of the body."

I caught her glancing down at my lap. I blushed and quickly covered myself with my hands.

She laughed again. Her laughter once again did not help.

"But then I saw you. You are so handsome and strong. I didn't want to lie to you. I–I'm sorry."

She jumped to her feet before I could tell her that it wasn't her fault. She started to run away, but I caught up to her quickly.

I grabbed her wrist and spun her to face me. I stood nearly a foot taller than her and had to look down into her eyes.

"It isn't your fault. Other people have controlled my whole life, Gisei. The monks at the monastery, Bodhi, Tsuyoi, even Suzaku–they all tell me what to do or how to think or how to feel. All because I am destined to be Animetown's great hero."

I didn't realize I was still holding her wrist and squeezing it in my anger. I let go and saw that I left a mark. I think I was more scared about that than Gisei.

She looked up at me.

"So now what?" she asked, rubbing her wrist.

"I'm sorry."

She smiled and made my insides squirm again. "It's okay. I know you didn't mean to hurt me." She stepped closer to me and tilted her head back to look into my face. "So now what?" She had a very faint smile curling at the edge of her mouth.

"Tsuyoi doesn't need to know everything." I ignored my body's nervous protesting and put my arms around Gisei's waist. "Just tell her I resisted you."

She bit her lower lip again. "Did you?"

I bent my neck down and kissed her. I closed my eyes and pulled her close against me. I don't know how long the embrace lasted, but it felt like an eternity. When I separated from Gisei, I looked into her eyes and smirked.

"Of course I did."

* * *

"Today we complete your final test, the Great Physical Trial," Tsuyoi said.

Another six months had passed in Kajiba. Suzaku and I were on speaking terms shortly after I told her that I was willing to ignore my hormones and focus on my training. Tsuyoi pushed me harder and never mentioned anything about Gisei, so I figured that we were hiding our relationship well.

My body became as well chiseled as any of the men in the village. Tsuyoi was the only one who was able to match me in one-on-one combat and even she became winded sooner than me. By the end of my training, she had me fighting two or three grown men at the same time just to keep me challenged.

I stood in front of her with Suzaku hovering proudly over my shoulder. Tsuyoi declared to the village that I was ready for my final challenge.

I eyed the assembled villagers and wondered what this Great Physical Trial would be. I thought maybe I would just have to fight the whole village at the same time. I couldn't think of a more difficult physical trial than that.

"You're going to forge a sword," Tsuyoi announced.

I scoffed. "I've been making swords for months. What's so hard about that?"

Tsuyoi looked to Suzaku who, I noticed, was holding the bag I had carried with me from her temple in Animetown. It contained the ashes I had collected from her egg room in the temple. She dropped the bag at my feet.

"You're going to make a sword with these."

I felt my eyebrows meet at the middle of my forehead. "With your ashes?"

Suzaku landed and looked up at me. "Yes. You can make a sword with them that is virtually indestructible. No one else can work with the material, so you have to do it."

Tsuyoi placed her hand on my shoulder. "You are an amazing fighter, Yoshi. You deserve an amazing weapon. A blade made with the ashes of Suzaku will be unlike any sword to ever exist." She pointed to the nearest forge in the village. "Get to work."

Still confused, I picked up the bag and went to the forge with Suzaku. The villagers had prepared the fires and the forge was ready to go. I placed the bag on an anvil and looked to Suzaku.

"Is this another one of those things you can't tell me how to do and I have to figure it out on my own?"

"Pretty much," Suzaku answered with a smile.

"I'm betting you don't even know," I ventured.

Suzaku scoffed. "Yeah, like I'm an idiot that will fall for that one, Yoshi. I have all the knowledge that my line has gained over the years. It passed down to me when I was reborn."

"So how long has your 'line' lived then?"

"Forever."

"Really? How does that even work?"

"Shouldn't you be focused on the task at hand, Yoshi?" she asked.

I turned back to the bag of ashes sitting on the anvil. She was right, but I hated to admit it to her. She already knew she was right anyway so it didn't do any good to acknowledge it. I figured I should just try something, so I perused the sword molds and picked out what I wanted.

"Compensating for something?" asked Suzaku, staring at the large mold I selected. The long blade was nearly as tall as me. The mold had never been used as far as I could tell. The metals we had in Kajiba weren't strong enough to obtain the durability needed to survive a battle intact with such a long blade.

"A Masamune," I said to no one in particular. "If your ashes are so amazing as a material, I should be able to make one with them."

"As long as you don't hurt yourself with it," the phoenix mocked.

I ignored her and set up the mold. I was used to pouring molten metals into the molds and letting them dry. I wasn't sure how to make the ashes into a workable material. I placed them into a clay pot and tried heating them in the forge.

"Are you seriously trying to melt them? The ashes of a phoenix?" Suzaku laughed. "Maybe you need to go back to Bodhi for more mental training."

I knew it was a long shot, but if there was something I did remember from my mind training it was that I should at least try the obvious first. I poured water into the container, the way I would mix water into the clay we used to make pots and weapon molds. The water immediately boiled and turned to steam.

"Ooh, thought you had it there," Suzaku offered.

"Do you ever say anything useful?" I replied.

"To you? Not really."

I groaned and looked into the pot. The ashes were unchanged from when I started working with them. The steam was still pouring from the pot and blasted my face. Beads of sweat fell from my forehead into the pot. I was amazed at what happened next.

The ashes responded to my sweat. They actually absorbed the salty water from my pores and became wet. My sweat didn't boil like the water. I shot a glance at Suzaku, who beamed at me.

"It needs my sweat?"

"Among other things."

I groaned as I thought about a common saying that the artisans and weaponsmiths would use in regards to their work. I couldn't count how many times I heard them talk about putting their "blood, sweat, and tears" into their work. I mentioned this to Suzaku.

"Even clichés start from an element of reality at some point in time," she said.

I used a cloth to drain as much sweat from my head as I could. The ashes thickened as I wrung the sweat into the jar. A small blade slice to my arm made providing blood for the jar a simple task.

"What about tears?" I asked Suzaku.

"What about them?"

"How do I get them out? I haven't cried since I was a kid."

"One might argue that you still are a kid," she began, "but I know what you mean." She looked thoughtful for a moment. "What if you think about your family and all the bad stuff that happened to you as a child?"

I shook my head. "All that does is make me angry. Don't you think I already think about that all the time?"

"Close your eyes," Suzaku commanded.

I listened to her and squeezed my eyes shut. I heard the flapping of wings and a small amount of struggle from the great phoenix. Then I felt an immense pain in my foot.

"*YEEOOW!*" I screamed.

I opened my eyes and looked down at a large metal anvil on my foot. It took four or five of the strongest men in Kajiba to move one of these anvils. Suzaku had picked one up and dropped it on my foot. The pain was worse than anything I had ever felt. A few tears streamed down my cheeks. Suzaku picked up the jar and added my tears to the mixture of ashes, sweat, and blood.

When she removed the anvil, I tried to punch her, but she flew into the air.

"You should be thanking me," she said.

"For dropping . . . an anvil . . . on my foot?" I sputtered.

"We got the tears!" she cried in defense of her actions.

I limped to the pot and jostled it. Somehow, the mixture looked very much like the molten metals I had worked at the forge in my training. I struggled to move with the pot. My foot was probably full of shattered bones.

Suzaku actually helped me position the mold so I could pour the mixture into it.

I set the mold aside and sat down. I didn't want to look at my foot and see what damage was done.

"Oh, it'll heal, you big baby," Suzaku said as she rested on the mold.

"Let me drop an anvil on your claw and see how you feel."

Suzaku scoffed. "Did you miss the part where I can pick the anvil up by myself?"

"I didn't know you were that strong."

"There's a lot you don't know about me, Yoshi." She smiled and tapped a talon on the sword mold. "Ding! Your sword is done."

I cracked open the mold and saw the finest looking blade I had ever witnessed. Lifting it from the mold, I took it to the village square, where Tsuyoi and some of the villagers waited to see what I had made.

"A Masamune?" Tsuyoi said with admiration. "That's the most beautiful blade I've ever seen, Yoshi." She observed my limp and looked at my injured foot. "What's with the foot?"

"Suzaku dropped an anvil on it."

"Ah," she said without judgment. "Yoshi, the village of Kajiba would be honored if you would allow us to craft the hilt and sheath for this blade."

"As would I, Tsuyoi."

The villagers took great care with the Masamune blade I had forged with Suzaku's ashes and my own blood, sweat, and tears. In about a week, I was prepared to journey to the last of the great senseis for my final warrior training. Tsuyoi made me some awful tasting elixir that she claimed would heal bones. Either my foot wasn't as injured as I first thought or it worked, because I was able to walk somewhat pain-free.

I made a point to pass along the location of the spirit trainer, Anatta, to Gisei before we left Kajiba. She promised that she would meet me there. I wish I had known at the time how bad of an idea that was.

Part Five: The Spirit Sensei

When Tsuyoi first told me that the third and final sensei lived alone at the top of Kajiba Mountain, I was annoyed. Even with my stronger body and increased endurance, there didn't seem to be any way to climb the mountain's sheer face. She said the only path up was on the opposite side and would take several weeks to reach by river then by land.

The pain in my foot returned and required an alternate form of travel. That and Gisei would need to travel the distance as well. She said it was worth it, but there had to be a better way.

"Carry me!" I cried to Suzaku as we stood at the base of the mountain.

"Excuse me?" she asked.

I grinned. "I'm sorry. Great Suzaku, most beautiful of birds and smartest creature in Animetown, can you please carry me to the top of the mountain?" The compliments tasted sour in my mouth but I knew she wanted to hear me ask her nicely, even if it was sarcastic.

"Well, in that case, sure."

One benefit to this method of travel was that I couldn't hear Suzaku during the trip as she flew us to the top of the mountain. In our last two travel sessions, she talked the whole time about how much things had changed in one hundred years. This used to be an orange grove. This village wasn't here before. It was like listening to an old woman ramble.

One detriment to traveling by flight, though, was that she had to carry me by my arms in her large talons. It didn't hurt but it wasn't exactly the most regal means of travel. Getting carried like a child in the talons of a giant bird was more comical than honorable.

We landed on a flat surface that jutted out from the main mountain. There was a cave entrance in the face of the rock and a narrow walkway that crept up the side of the mountain to the platform on which Suzaku and I were standing. This was the path Gisei would take when she came to visit me.

"Suzaku," I said while rubbing the feeling back into my arms. "Can I ask you a question so I don't sound like an idiot to Anatta?"

"I'm not sure if any question you ask me can prevent that from happening, but sure."

"What's the difference between the mind and the spirit? I get why body is different but the two of them seem to be the same."

"Actually, mind and body are closer in relation than mind and spirit." Suzaku landed and tucked her wings into her side.

I noted how she was still growing and she had to have a ten-foot wingspan by now. I couldn't even think of a bird to compare her to anymore. She was larger than any bird I had ever heard of, let alone seen.

"You there?"

She must have grown a lot during our long time in Kajiba but I was too focused on my training and Gisei to notice. "Yeah, sorry. I just realized how big you are. Are you done growing yet?"

Suzaku held out her wings and looked herself over. "Almost. So did you want me to answer your question or no?"

"Yes, I'm sorry. How are mind and body closer to the same than mind and spirit?"

"Because the two of them are still physical. You train them by working them. The mind is just a muscle, no different than your arms or legs. You push it to its limits and it strengthens to keep up."

"And the spirit? What is it?"

"Something less tangible. Some call it a soul. Some call it consciousness. Some call it self. Either way, you can't just give it a puzzle or make it fight to train it."

"So how do you train it?"

Suzaku opened her beak to answer but paused. I saw a look on her face that I had never seen in my phoenix companion before. I knew before she even said it what her answer was. "I don't know."

I stared in shock. Suzaku reached out with one of her giant wings and pushed my mouth closed. I hadn't realized it was open.

"Can we go inside and find out now?" she asked in annoyance.

I smiled and nodded. Just like I never needed to tell her that she was right, I didn't need to point out that she had no answers for once. I pocketed the memory in the back of my mind.

We entered the cave and followed a faint light to the back. We were only a few hundred feet inside when we came to a man sitting next to a fire. He sat quietly staring into the flames. He was bald but didn't seem that old. He wore the same orange robes as the monks from Suzaku temple.

I cleared my throat to let him know we were there. He made no indication that he heard me. I turned to Suzaku, who shrugged her wings. I sat down next to the monk, who I assumed was Anatta.

Suzaku clearly felt cramped in the small cave and made her way back to the landing outside the entrance where she could stretch out her wings without causing any damage.

I looked at the monk again before curiosity led me to stare into the fire. The flame was nothing special, as far I could tell. It just looked like an ordinary fire to me. I couldn't understand why the monk was so entranced. I sat down next to Anatta and tried to emulate him. It seemed the most logical thing to do given the circumstances.

I'm not sure how long I sat at the fire. At first, I just focused on watching the flames lick at the space above. The colors slowly changed from red to orange to yellow, as the flame got closer to the source of combustion.

I could smell the burning wood at the source and hear the small crackles from the fire. The heat was intense on my face, causing beads of sweat to form and quickly run down my skin. I even tasted some of the ash and smoke that rose from the burning wood.

Thinking back to my training in the Buddhist monastery, I attempted to ignore the sensory overload of the fire and instead meditate with my mind's eye. I tried not to focus on the perceptions that were being enhanced by my close proximity to a source that hit all five of my senses with such intensity.

"Yoshi!" I heard a quiet shout from the entrance to the cave.

I snapped out of my trance and felt a wave of vertigo hit me. I turned to the sound of my name and saw Suzaku's head at the cave entrance. I looked at the monk, who seemed just as oblivious to the world as when I first sat down. I rose and felt tightness in my back and cramping in my legs.

"How long was I sitting there, Suzaku?"

"A few hours."

"Wow." I rubbed the feeling into my legs and left the monk and fire to their staring contest. "What's wrong?"

"A bird just delivered a message for you." As I reached the entrance to the cave, Suzaku pointed to a very harried carrier bird. "You've got some explaining to do."

"Why? What is the message?"

Suzaku held out a message in her wingtip. "Pirates have kidnapped Gisei and say they will return her if you pay a ransom."

I felt my throat close a bit.

"Why would they contact you, Yoshi?"

The phoenix didn't expect an answer. She already knew.

She sighed. "Yoshi, you lied to me and Tsuyoi about Gisei? Did you get Gisei to lie to her family and village also?"

A wave of anger rose up in me. "And did you know that she was sent to try to test my body? To see if I could control myself?" Suzaku nodded. "So you lied to me, then?"

"Not really lie," she started, "more like withheld information." She grinned.

"I'm not smiling, Suzaku. Ever since you chose to hatch for me, other people have controlled my life. Now the woman I love is in danger because we had to hide our feelings for one another to keep from being ripped apart by my destiny. I'm going after her, you know."

I heard a yawn at my back. Anatta was standing at the entrance of the cave. He covered his mouth with one hand and waved lightly with the other. "What's up?" he asked.

Suzaku motioned toward Anatta with her head. "You can't leave. You have to finish your spirit training."

"Finish what? Learning how to stare at a fire and strengthen my spirit like this old guy?"

Anatta responded, "I was actually just sleeping. And I'm not that old. When did you get here?"

I slumped my shoulders. "Wait, so staring into the fire wasn't some sort of test to see if I could strip myself of my senses and remind myself that they are not what makes me who I am?"

The monk's eyes perked up. "No, but that's a really good idea." He pointed at me and looked at Suzaku. "He's pretty smart."

"Hardly," Suzaku replied.

"Look, I don't care about my training, Suzaku. Master Anatta, I apologize, but even Suzaku said she has no idea how to train my spirit to be stronger. I can't test it with mind games or physical trials. I can't break it and rebuild it like my brain or my body."

I felt my emotions welling up. I was angry at being controlled. I was scared and sad that Gisei was in trouble. I was furious that pirates, who had already done so much damage to people I cared about, were the cause. I made up my mind to leave immediately.

"Maybe the real test of spirit is that I just have to live my life and trust that every experience I have is a small test that makes me who I am meant to be. What if life itself is the Great Spiritual Trial?"

I began trudging down the small path on the side of the mountain that led to the base. I heard Anatta say something but didn't hear what it was and didn't really care. I had to save Gisei from the pirates.

Part Six: The Revenge

I only made it a few hundred feet down the narrow sliver of a path from Anatta's cave before I heard the flapping of giant wings behind me. Suzaku flew next to me as I moved as quickly as I could without falling to my death.

"You passed," Suzaku said.

"Passed what?" I asked, kicking a few stones off the mountain.

"Your spirit training. Anatta said that you were exactly right and learned the lesson faster than any student he's ever had."

I stopped. I didn't realize I had learned a lesson.

Suzaku curled her beak into a smile. "That is why your spirit training comes last. It never is actually over. You realized that right away."

I shrugged and began walking again. I was annoyed that I had to come up to the mountain and leave Gisei to learn such a simple lesson.

"Not going to ask me?" she questioned.

I kept walking.

"Fine, I will tell you. Yes, I knew that was the lesson you needed to learn."

I stopped walking. "Just like you knew how to solve the Color Cube and you knew Gisei was part of the test and you knew how to make your ashes into a workable material for forging, right?"

"Yes."

"And even though you're supposed to be my companion, you've never helped me with any of these things."

"If I told you the answers to any of these things, how would you have learned them? Think of who you are today because of the trials you've been through in the last two years. You're a true warrior now, Yoshi."

I allowed myself to smile faintly. A compliment from Suzaku was rare. I made eye contact with the hovering giant phoenix and knew she was right. I quickly reverted back to thoughts of Gisei.

"Are you going to stop me from rescuing Gisei?"

Suzaku shook her head. "Why would I do that?" She smirked. I sensed a little more than just her normal snarkiness in the bird's face. "Warriors are trained to fight bad guys. Let's go wreck some pirates."

I smiled and leaped off the side of the mountain. Suzaku caught me by the arms with her claws and flew us both down to the river. We began our search for the pirates responsible for Gisei's kidnapping.

A quick stop in Kajiba led us to more information. Gisei had snuck out the night after I left and started making her way to the other side of the mountain. Pirates on the river attacked the boat she stowed away in and took her captive. Chichi, Gisei's father, begged me to return her safely to Kajiba. I vowed to do so.

Suzaku and I learned the pirates who captured Gisei were a small band of the main pirate force and made berth from Kaizoku Island, the only one of the Pirate Isles that fell within the outskirts of Animetown's section of the Toonopolis Ocean. Suzaku flew us to the island without any further delay.

We landed on the beach near a mid-size pirate ship moored to a makeshift pier. Suzaku stood next to me and looked excited. I was surprised.

"You look like you're ready to fight as much as I am, Suzaku."

"It's been a while since I've had a good battle with a hero by my side."

My cheeks warmed.

"No sarcasm, Yoshi. You may be an idiot, but I am proud to stand by you in battle."

"Then let's get to it."

The pirates weren't difficult to track. The boot prints on the beach led through a sparsely treed forest to a shantytown not far from the beach. The dilapidated buildings showed signs that they were only used occasionally, such as the obvious lack of attention to repairing broken windows and shoddy roofs.

I stood in the center of the town and shouted at the top of my lungs, "I demand to speak to your leader." The laughter and jeers I received through the doors of the buildings weren't what I'd anticipated.

One of the doors creaked open and a large, white man stepped out. He wore a red bandana, sailing boots, and a white, long-sleeved shirt. The hilt of a rapier and the butt of a pistol peeked out of the red sash at his waist.

"And who be ye, boy?" barked the scraggly-bearded pirate.

I faced the man. "I am Yoshi, sole survivor of the pirate raids on Hiun and Higeki of Animetown. I demand the release of Gisei of Kajiba immediately."

"Fancy that, eh? Well, I be Chuck Colson, first mate to Boreas, King of the Pirates."

He whistled. A rumble of activity in the buildings suggested the whistle was a call to action for the other pirates. Very quickly, a motley mixture of scoundrels surrounded Suzaku and I.

"Lookee here, lads. Looks like we missed one when we sacked . . . what was the name of your hometown again, Yosh?" He grinned and showed off a mouth that was missing many teeth.

I realized he was baiting me in an attempt to anger me. Tsuyoi would use this technique often to try

** 91 **

to get me to forget about the training and fight with anger. Sometimes, she said, it was a good thing. Other times, it would get me killed. I knew this was no time to be fighting with blind anger.

"I have no desire to play your games, fiend." I unsheathed my Masamune from behind me and held out its long, gleaming blade. I positioned my feet for mobility, preparing for an attack from all sides.

Chuck Colson brought a hand to his heart. "Ya hurt me feelins, lad. As for yer lass? We changed our minds on the ransom. King Boreas decided to take her home with 'im. Thinkin' he wants a new nursemaid for his wee daughter." He laughed and pulled his pistol. "Guess ye can leave."

He fired a shot directly at me.

I don't remember how I did it, but time seemed to slow down as I watched the bullet fly towards me. I stepped back and sliced at the projectile with my sword. The Masamune cut it in two like an apple, each half falling harmlessly to either side of me. I smiled at the pirate.

"Howdja? Whatdja? Who?"

Suzaku rose to the air. "Whendja? Wheredja? Whydja?" she added. She cast a large shadow over the pirate square, and spoke proudly. "You stand before Yoshi of Higeki, hero of Animetown. There is no greater warrior in our land and he is here to protect his people from the likes of you."

The pirates collectively moved their gazes back and forth between the giant phoenix flying above them and the swordsman that just cut down a bullet in mid-air. Most of the pirates were paralyzed, not knowing whether they should fight or run.

Suzaku read their emotions the same way I did. She taunted them. "You can run now, if you'd like."

Many of the pirates scattered like rats in the daylight. Chuck Colson was the only one who didn't move. He still held his pistol in the position from which he had shot at me. I walked towards him and he fell to his knees.

I pointed my sword at him. "Where are Boreas and the girl you kidnapped near Kajiba?"

"D-deeper into the island through the thicker part of the forest. Boreas has a private house there."

I nodded and turned my back to the pirate and motioned for Suzaku to follow me. Colson's breathing grew heavier and his bulky boots scuffled along the wooden porch of his rundown building.

I sighed.

"Are you really going to try to sneak up on me with your heavy wheezing and clumsy feet?"

I heard him fall back to his knees.

"I didn't think so."

Suzaku and I left the pirates otherwise unharmed. They weren't the ones I was after and would hardly present a challenging fight. We passed through the town, feeling the hidden eyes of the pirates watching us leave.

As we entered the thick part of the forest, I caught a familiar sight that made me reach for the hilt of my blade: a figure clad in all black. A voice I hadn't heard since I was a child chilled me. "Do not be alarmed. I am not here to fight you."

The ninja stood in front of me with his hands held so his palms faced out, showing me that he was unarmed.

I narrowed my eyes and spoke deeply. "But perhaps I am here to fight you, ninja."

"I'm not sure you want to fight one to whom you owe your life, Yoshi."

I grasped the hilt of my sword more firmly.

"I have heard of your training and deeds since I last saw you, child. Do you remember me?"

"Naito," I said. "You were with the ninja leader, Kunoichi, the night Hiun was destroyed. You are the reason I was twice left without a home as a child and you claim I owe you my life?"

"Yes," he began, "I used my ninjitsu to block Kunoichi's fireball that night. Do you remember the tree that fell on you?"

I didn't give him an answer but he took my silence as agreement.

"She didn't realize it at the time. I am not sure she ever did."

"Why did you save me?"

"We ninja are assassins, not murderers. Kunoichi allowed her hatred for the pirates to drive us into a pointless war with many innocent deaths. Now that I lead the ninja, the war is over."

Suzaku chimed in for the first time. "Then why are you here on Kaizoku Island?"

Naito paused in thought for a moment. Then he responded, "I was delivering a peace offering and truce agreement to Boreas. The Ninja-Pirate War has ended."

"What happened to Kunoichi?" I asked.

"Dead," Naito replied curtly.

I released my hold on my Masamune's hilt and looked down. I was happy that one of my revenge targets was dead, but I was also upset that I wasn't able to be the one to kill her.

I hadn't noticed Naito sneak beside me until he put a hand on my shoulder. "I think you'll find Boreas a changed man, Yoshi," he said. "Age has wizened him and life has presented him with new purpose. You should talk to him."

I shook off Naito's hold on my shoulder. "If what you say is true, I do owe you my life. That does not change my opinion of both ninjas and pirates. You are all murderers and need to pay for your crimes."

I read sadness in Naito's black eyes. "Suit yourself, hero, but someone has to end the cycle. Let it be you and your legend shall be great." In a puff of smoke, Naito vanished into the woods.

Suzaku looked at me, and I saw concern in her eyes. "He's right, you know."

I recalled Bikkhu Soohei saying something similar to me when I was a boy.

"Violence begets violence," he lectured the children at the monastery. "The truly strong find ways to end conflict without continuing to turn the wheel."

I shook my head of such impractical notions. The violence would stop when one was stronger than the rest. That's how you end the cycle. What did a monk who never had to fight these battles know about it?

I strode toward the Pirate King's house. In a cleared section of the woods, I found it. The door stood open. I entered and found the man I had waited twelve years to see again. His hair was a mixture of the blond I remembered and white. He had lines of age on his face and around his eyes, but the brightness of his green irises hadn't faded over the years.

Sitting on his lap was a little girl, about four or five years old. She had blond hair and green eyes like his. Maybe it was because of those eyes, but I hated her immediately.

"Hi, Yoshi. Naito told me ye was coming."

"Save your words, scum," I snarled. "I am not here to talk to you. You killed my parents. You killed countless innocent people in your plundering and pillaging. You deserve to die." I unsheathed my sword and held it tightly.

Boreas didn't disagree with anything I said. He placed the little girl on the ground and patted her head. "Zephyr, why don't ye run along into the bedroom and play with those nice dolls Naito gave you." Zephyr looked scared of my sword and seemed please to leave the room. She obeyed and left through a door bchind Boreas.

He stood up with much effort, his joints clearly not working as well as they once did. He kneeled in front of me and bared his chest.

"I don't deny any of those accusations. I've been a bad man. I beg of ye forgiveness and ask that I have a chance to redeem meself through teaching me daughter how to be a better person than I was and raise her to lead the pirates in a new direction."

"Why should I believe anything you say? Your pirate spawn will be just as evil as you." I felt rage growing inside me. My heart rate was increasing and my skin was warming. I felt like I must have been turning red.

"I'm not asking you to believe me, Yoshi. I'm asking you to give me a chance to prove that a wicked man can change."

I glanced at Suzaku, who gave a nod, approving of the pirate's words. I turned back to Boreas.

"Where is Gisei?"

Boreas looked down at the ground. "I hate to inform you that she is dead."

I looked at Suzaku again, my eyes wide with anger. Then I stabbed the Pirate King through the chest with my blade.

"*YOSHI!*" Suzaku cried as the pirate's eyes widened in shock and pain.

He gasped, a trickle of blood escaping the corner of his mouth, and fell over.

I spat on him. "No amount of action can undo your evil past. Death is your only release." I pulled my blade free from the Pirate King's dead body and looked at Suzaku, who had tears in her eyes. "He was a wicked man and I wished for his death for twelve long years."

Suzaku wiped her eyes with her feathers. "You were destined to be great. You were supposed to be a hero."

"I never said I was a hero. You did. I wanted to be strong enough to get revenge. Now I am." I stepped over Boreas's body and began walking toward the door in the back of the room.

"Where are you going?" Suzaku screeched.

"To end the pirate spawn's line."

Suzaku rose up in anger and nearly knocked me over with the gusts from her powerful wings. She flew to block my path.

"I will not allow you to kill an innocent child, Yoshi. She has done no wrong."

"Her blood is tainted with pirate blood."

Suzaku swung at me with a wing. I held up my sword to defend myself. The two weapons bounced off one another. The blade had no effect on the phoenix.

"People are not born evil, Yoshi, regardless of how evil their parents are. It is their surroundings that make them evil or . . ." She searched for words and looked at me, "heartless."

My blood was too hot with anger and satisfaction at avenging my parents and Gisei to listen to her. "Fine," I spat. "Let's go then. My work here is done."

I turned and stepped once again over the dead body of the pirate who had killed my mother and father. I kicked him for good measure along the way. I heard no motion behind me to suggest that Suzaku was following. I turned at the door and saw she hadn't moved.

"You coming, companion?"

"No," she said quietly.

"I thought we were connected by destiny?" I mocked.

"No, Yoshi, we are not." She sat slumped, not looking as graceful as she did when flying. "Destiny isn't really predetermined. I thought that if I guided you, led you down the right paths, that you would become the great warrior I felt you were capable of being."

"I am a great warrior, Suzaku."

"But you are no hero."

I pointed to the dead Pirate King on the ground. "I defeated an evil man to protect future innocents from suffering."

"You killed an old, defenseless man who was pleading for his life on behalf of his daughter."

I smirked, "You say potato, I say—"

"Stop it. I'm staying here, Yoshi, to look after Zephyr. Maybe she'll be able to live the life her father envisioned for her. Someone has to stop the cycle of anger, death, and revenge."

I felt a little sting of pain. Suzaku had been with me for years and was the closest thing in the world I had to a friend. The sting of righteousness hit me more strongly, though. "Fine. I am going back to Animetown to receive my hero's welcome."

"You are no hero," she repeated. "You are anti-hero. You are anchihiiroo."

I shrugged at Suzaku and turned away from her again. I began my trek back to Animetown alone.

"Anchihiiroo," I said out loud. "I can live with that name."

Part Seven: The Shadow Man

Despite Suzaku protesting against the way I enacted my revenge on the Pirate King, I received a hero's welcome in Animetown as stories of my heroics against the pirates made their way through the rumor chain. I was hailed as the hero who ended the Ninja-Pirate War. It wasn't entirely honest, but I felt the truth was no excuse for letting Naito and Boreas get the credit.

When I made my way back to Suzaku's temple several years later, Bikkhu Soohei greeted me with a smile. "Where is Suzaku?" he asked.

"She decided she was better off playing babysitter to pirate spawn than remaining with me," I answered.

Soohei looked at me suspiciously.

I shrugged. "We don't need her, Bikkhu. I am the strong warrior that I set out to be when I left this temple six years ago."

"You certainly look like it," a male said from behind me.

I smiled at the sound of Yuki's voice. I turned to see my albino friend from the temple.

"You're monstrous."

** 101 **

I looked down at myself and compared my physique to Yuki's. I was always bigger than him but I hadn't realized how muscular and large I had become during my warrior training. I generally only had Suzaku to compare myself to and she grew faster than I did.

"What is that?" I asked, pointing to a robotic frame standing on four legs next to him.

"It's a prototype of the artificial intelligence I told you about years ago. I'm programming it to act like a dog." He patted what I guessed was the head of the robot. "Sit, Wan-Wan." The hind legs of the robot frame bent and sat down just like a dog. "It's going well!"

I laughed. "Only you would come up with something like this, Yuki."

"Nice sword," Yuki added.

I unsheathed my Masamune and let it catch the sunlight to make it shine. "Forged from the ashes of Suzaku," I explained.

"Where is she anyway?"

"I'll explain later."

Yuki eyed me with the same suspicious glare as Soohei. "So, hero, what's your plan now that you have fulfilled your destiny and become Animetown's hero?"

"Do tell," added Soohei.

I rubbed my chin. I hadn't actually thought of that before. I was so sated with my vengeance against Boreas that I didn't know what I planned on doing next. I had become a warrior to get revenge. Now that the revenge was complete, I didn't know the next step.

"I guess I'll just be a hero-for-hire," I concluded.

"For hire?" asked Soohei.

"Sure. Why not? Who said that heroes had to work for free?" I smiled.

Yuki and Soohei didn't return the smiles. Yuki said, "I didn't think becoming Animetown's hero meant you would become a mercenary."

"Hey, I still will fight bad guys and save people and the like. Mercenaries work for anyone who pays. I'll just work for people who need me to help them. It isn't any different from paying a blacksmith for his skills in sword-making, or a tinkerer," I pointed at Yuki, "to do whatever it is you do."

Yuki and Soohei protested my establishment of a hero-for-hire business in Animetown but I did it anyway. It turned out that the job was very lucrative. I didn't always work for money, and I didn't always complete my tasks exactly as my clients asked.

"I didn't want you to kill him," one whiner said. "I just wanted my cows back."

"You got your cows, didn't you?" I replied.

"And a dead neighbor!"

"Consider it a bonus, free of charge."

I established myself as the preeminent hero in Animetown, just like my fake destiny said I would. I did it on my terms, however. If I was destined to become a great hero and had no control over that aspect of my life, at least I would make a profit from my abilities so graciously taught to me by the senseis.

Suzaku never returned to the temple. Over the years, there were rumors of a giant red bird on some of the pirate ships that still sailed the waters outside of Animetown's territory. No pirates came into Animetown on my watch.

For ten years, I continued my hero-for-hire business. Everything changed the day a mysterious shadowy figure appeared in front of me.

"Anchihiiroo," rasped the shadow man. He was covered in smoky wisps and shadows, and I couldn't really make out any true form other than a vague human shape in the smoke.

"Smoking is bad for you," I said to the man.

"Funny," said the shadow man in a deadpan.

"What can I do for you, sir? Ma'am? What should I call you?"

"I have come to be known as Shadowy Figure to the residents of Toonopolis."

"Not very original of a name there, Mr. Figure."

"Says the man who goes by the name Anchihiiroo?"

I smiled at his rebuttal.

"However, it is not what you can do for me that brings me here, Yoshi. It is what I can do for you."

He caught my attention with his raspy words and his usage of my real name. I stood up and realized that I towered over him. His shadows grew so he was the same height as me.

Shadowy Figure continued. "I've heard your story throughout Animetown. You hate having to be a hero when all you wanted to do was get revenge for your family, right?"

"I make do."

"How would you like to make your own path and decide who you want to be instead of following someone else's vision?"

"I've already done that."

Shadowy Figure laughed. It was a grating, shrill laugh that made my arm hair stand on end. Something in the laugh made me want to know what he was talking about. I asked him to explain. What he told me was amazing.

At first, I thought he was crazy. He told me that Toonopolis was actually populated by ideas and thoughts of people from a place called Earth and other universes that were filled with sentient beings. All the people in Animetown and Toonopolis, myself included, were just creations from the minds of these beings.

"They're like gods?" I asked.

"Hardly," he said. "But that's not important. What is important is that there exists an invisible thread from you back to your creator on Earth. You can follow that thread back to him and change who you are from within that person's mind."

"Why should I believe you?" I asked him.

"Because I have been there. I have seen it done. I learned about the technique from a woman in the Black Light District. I taught it to a boy in Supercity. You can change yourself. I promise you that."

What he said still came across as crazy. If I were to believe him, I would have to accept that someone else—even above Suzaku, Bodhi, and Tsuyoi—was really pulling my strings like I was a marionette.

"So this creator, if he exists, is the real reason I have suffered so much? The loss of my family? The death of my love, Gisei? My phoenix abandoning me?"

"Maybe. Probably. Your creator is definitely the reason you still feel like you have to be a hero, even if you want to be a villain. The creators don't necessarily control every aspect of your life, just your basic programming."

I sat back down and figured that I had nothing to lose by at least trying it. If the Shadowy Figure was pulling a prank on me, I could always just kill him in retaliation.

At first, it was very difficult to be able to focus. I thought to my meditation techniques learned at the temple and from my various teachers. With time and focus, I learned his technique for finding the string and was surprised to find that it was real. I relished in the irony that the lessons taught to me by those who strove to force me to become a hero were the key to erase that path of destiny.

I traveled with my mind across the string and found myself inside the mind of my creator. It is very hard to explain the experience to someone who has never done it. Inside his mind, I was able to shape his vision of me. I removed the portion of my personality that compelled me to be a hero.

When I returned to my body, Shadowy Figure was giggling. "How do you feel, Anchihiiroo?"

"Call me Han'Eiyuu," I replied, a grin spreading across my face. I felt so different. There was no longer a conscience tugging on me to do good deeds. I felt totally free, like I could do whatever I wanted.

"Well, Han'Eiyuu, it is time for you to pay me for your freedom," Shadowy Figure said, his giggles gone.

"Pay?" I questioned.

"Don't worry," the shadow man said, "I don't want money. I have another target to teach this Rogue technique to and I must be on my way. I am planning on changing Toonopolis forever, Han'Eiyuu, and you Rogues are just the beginning."

"And your payment?"

"You will likely be meeting an Outsider to Toonopolis soon, a young man who calls himself Gemini. He will want to defeat you to get to me. I am not ready to deal with him yet. I need you to stall him here."

"Shall I eliminate him?" I pointed to my Masamune.

"You won't be able to but I need him alive anyway. As strong as you are, Gemini has powers you can't even fathom since he is one of these creators whose mind you just saw. He is strong in ways you can't imagine. Slow him down. That is all I ask of you."

"It is a promise, Shadowy Figure."

"Good boy," he replied.

He wafted through the door of my house and left Animetown. I decided to experiment with my newfound freedom and lack of conscience by terrorizing some of the local townsfolk. They were completely caught off guard. I decided not to kill any of them but it was fun taking what I wanted and seeing the fear in their eyes. Causing other people pain helped to make me feel better about my own.

I found myself in the center of Animetown and looked up at Suzaku's temple. I balled up my fists and shouted at the temple, causing the few remaining people who weren't shuttered inside their homes to flee. "You think you're better than me, Suzaku?"

I charged at the temple and kicked in the door. The orange-robed monks cowered in fear at me. I made my way through the temple, destroying anything that got in my way. I found myself in front of the wooden door with the phoenix's picture painted on it. I sliced it in half with the blade made from the ashes that were once scattered on the floor of Suzaku's egg room.

My rage at Suzaku's abandonment finally started to subside as I stood inside the room.

"Yoshi!" cried Bikkhu Soohei from the door.

I looked back at the old monk and sneered. "This is my temple now, Soohei."

"What has gotten into you?"

"I am making my own destiny now. No monks or senseis or legendary birds or creators telling me what to do."

My eyes felt open wide and wild with power. Soohei simply backed away and left. I established Suzaku's old temple as my own after kicking out the monks.

Not long after, I heard from the villagers that a teenage boy dressed in lime green and fuchsia clothing was asking about me. I made my way to the roof of Suzaku Temple to survey Animetown from my perch.

Part Eight: The Present

Here I stand, wearing nothing but a pair of samurai pants and my Masamune on my back. I rest my hand on the top-most spire of the temple that once served to worship and prepare a warrior to represent Suzaku and be her companion. I have full control over my own life and my own future for the first time.

Shadowy Figure tells me that this child is coming to defeat me and make me follow my creator's original idea for my personality, despite how illogical it is. The shadow man tells me that Gemini is strong in ways that I can't imagine. He cannot be stronger than me. He cannot be faster than me. He cannot defeat the sword I forged with my own hands from phoenix ashes.

I wait and I smile. I will defeat this Outsider and set my sights on greater things. It feels so good to be free. I feel the air changing. It feels like battle weather.

I can't wait.

How To Create A Villain
or
Let Sleeping Candemons Lie

Author Note:

This is the first short story I wrote featuring side characters from the Toonopolis Files books. The

Candemon, who was one of the "big bads" in *Toonopolis: Gemini*, was such a fun character that I wanted to go back in time and add in a little more history between he, Roy G. Biv, and Princess Polipo. The result was a fun sweet sixteen story that shows sometimes you should just leave people alone when they ask.

This story was first published in *Wild Cards* in November 2013 by Vampirical Lyrical. It was later re-edited by A.F.E. Smith.

How To Create A Villain

"**H**ello? Are you in there?" Roy G. Biv called into the darkness of the monster's cave at the base of Marshmallow Mountain.

"No!" The monster's hollow voice echoed in the cave entrance.

"Then who just answered?"

"It's a recording–"

"Oh, come on, Candemon," Roy interrupted. "Do we really have to go through that gag? Can you just come talk to me?"

Roy heard the Candemon shuffling to his feet. He took a few steps back from the mouth of the cave and nervously adjusted his rainbow-colored bow tie. He forced a smile as the monster emerged from the darkness. The Candemon's pupil-less hard-candy eyes stared straight ahead.

"It's a beautiful day!" Roy cried. "Are you coming to the party at my castle?"

"What party?" he replied.

"I mailed you an invitation last week." Roy pointed a finger at the mailbox outside the cave that had C. Demon written on it in rainbow colors. The 'o' in demon was written as a little, red heart. "Um, you didn't have a mailbox so I made one for you. Then I put the invitation in it."

The Candemon walked awkwardly toward the mailbox on its candy-bar legs. He raised his candy-cane arms in the air . . .

SMASH!

. . . and destroyed the mailbox. "I hate parties," the Candemon said in his unique, empty-sounding voice. He turned back to the cave and walked back inside. The entrance of the cave framed his candy-apple head, making it look like the Candemon was wearing the mountain as a hat.

Roy giggled at the mental image. The Frankensteinian candy monster turned back to Roy and tilted his head to the side. "Is something funny?"

"Erm, no?" Roy replied. "But, how can you hate parties?"

"I've never been invited to one."

Roy heard a tinge of sadness in the Candemon's voice and grew hopeful. "But you just were! By me!"

The Candemon scratched its head with one of its candy-cane arms. He glanced at the shattered mailbox. "Why?"

"Because you live on my Candy Island! I want everyone on Candy Island to be able to have fun and be happy."

"But why now? You've had other parties."

Roy looked up at the Candemon. He had to, considering the monster was over twice Roy's height. Roy felt his gaze fall on the upside-down gummy-bear that served as the Candemon's torso. Something about the gummy bear's face serving as the Candemon's crotch always bothered Roy a little bit. The gummy bear's dead eyes looked just as vacant as the monster's proper ones.

"My eyes are up here," the Candemon said.

Roy didn't realize that he was staring at the gummy-bear face and quickly raised his eyes to the candy-apple head instead. "Sorry," he mumbled.

The Candemon crossed his arms over his chest. "And what fun and happiness is there for me, Roy?" Roy looked at the Candemon more intently. "And stop feeling sorry for me. I can feel your pity when you look at me."

He was right; Roy had always felt sorry for the Candemon, even though many of the other residents of Toonopolis feared and hated the creature.

"I'm sorry." Roy reached into his pocket and retrieved a handful of jellybeans. He offered a white one to the Candemon. "Jellybean? Freshly picked from the forest."

The Candemon reared back. "Two problems with that, Rainbow-Boy," he said. "Problem the first: me eating candy is pretty much cannibalism. Problem B: I hate the white ones because I always end up with nasty buttered popcorn."

"Oh, I guess . . . hey, wait a minute?" Roy sputtered as he realized the conflicting information within the Candemon's problems.

The Candemon laughed.

Roy's eyes opened in surprise. He had never heard the Candemon laugh before. Granted, it was a bit of a creepy, echo-y laugh, but a laugh nonetheless. Roy laughed too. "So you'll come to the party, then?"

The Candemon reached out with one of its arms. Roy flinched as the Candemon playfully flicked Roy's gnome hat to the ground. "We'll call it a maybe," the monster replied.

Roy picked up his hat and smiled. After placing his hat back on, he waved his fingers at the shattered mailbox. A stream of rainbows flew from Roy's hand and the mailbox was magically restored. "Bring your invitation."

Roy skipped away from the Candemon's cave happily, feeling hopeful that the Candemon might finally be able to join the rest of Candy Island's citizens in celebration. Now he just had to tell Princess Polipo that she was going to have a special guest at her Sweet Sixteen party.

* * *

"But Princess, you need to keep wet or your tentacles will dry out," said one of Polipo's royal guards.

"It's my party and I'll dry if I want to!" Polipo replied.

Roy heard the tail end of the conversation between the octonoid princess and her guard. He sighed. It sounded as though the Princess was continuing to be very demanding. She was standing on a stage in the center of Taffy Towers in a pink gown. The Rainbow PEZ Road ran underneath the stage and to Roy's throne behind it. She looked almost like a regular girl because her tentacles only barely poked out of the bottom. Roy felt her stare when she spied him. It was not a pleasant stare.

"Roy! Where have you been?!"

"Princess," her guard started, "you should not be impolite to Roy. It's rude to ask about his personal business."

"It's my party and I'll pry if I want to!" she replied.

The guard sighed and mouthed 'I'm sorry' to Roy. "Don't worry, Cal, it's okay," Roy said. "You really should wear something that will not get ruined when you get wet, Princess. You'll get cooked out here in the sun."

"It's my party and I'll fry–" her eyes drifted away from Roy and her face grew red.

Roy followed her stare. She was looking at an ice cream sculpture that was being carted in by a few of the party's caterers. Roy was impressed by the size and detail. It looked exactly like Princess Polipo, down to the pink fondant coloring her tentacles. Roy felt a breeze as the princess ran past him toward the sculpture.

"I'm really sorry, Roy," the guard said out loud. "Don't worry about it, Cal."

"Um, I'm Ceph. Cal is my brother."

Roy felt his ears warm. "I'm so sorry Ceph! I always get you two mixed up!"

Ceph narrowed his eyes and pressed his lips close together. He looked angry. "Are you saying all octonoids look the same?!"

Roy took a step back. "No . . . I just . . . you and Cal . . ."

"Oh stop it, brother." Roy turned and saw an identical-looking octonoid guard behind him. Ceph's twin brother Cal looked annoyed. "We really don't have time for this."

Ceph broke into a laugh and patted Roy on the shoulder. "My brother's right, Roy. We have to make sure everything is perfect for Polipo," he said with a bit of venom in his voice. "Can you keep an eye on Princess Pain-in-the-butt for a moment?"

"Sure Ceph. I have big news for her. A special guest!" Roy gave a thumbs-up to the twin guards as they walked away. He found Princess Polipo giving the ice cream sculptors an earful.

"—And my nose isn't that big! And my hair is chestnut, not brown! You are ruining my party!"

"Um, Princess," Roy called.

"What?" she cried over her shoulder. "Roy, these idiots are ruining everything. This is supposed to be the best party ever. All of my friends from Underwater City High are going to be so jealous. It's supposed to be epic!" She pointed a finger at the people holding the ice cream copy of Polipo. "They hate me. They want my party to suck!"

Roy shooed the caterers away and drew Polipo's attention. "I'll make sure they fix it, Princess. Don't worry."

"Good."

"Now can you let me modify your dress so you won't dry out? It will look exactly the same, I promise."

The princess rolled her eyes. "I guess."

Roy waved his hand, sending rainbows to encircle Princess Polipo. He wiggled his fingers and then threw his hands in the air, the rainbows flying into the sky as he did. Polipo looked exactly the same.

"Feel that?" he asked. "I added some magic mist into the fabric on the inside of your dress to help keep your tentacles moist." Polipo swirled in her dress, allowing the hem to spin in the air. She actually looked like she was going to smile. Roy didn't hold his breath.

"I have a surprise for you," said Roy. "You're going to have a special guest for the party."

"Ooh! Did Daddy get The Flatkey Boys to perform for me?!"

"Er, not exactly. But you will have a guest no one else has ever had. It's—"

BAHWOOOO!

Roy was interrupted by a trumpet blast from one of the royal guards. The sound of an octonoid conch shell was unmistakable. One blast of the trumpet called the octonoid guards.

BAHWOOOO!

Roy asked Polipo, "What does two conch blasts mean?"

"An attack," Polipo said. She yawned and shrugged her shoulders.

"But who would be attacking your part—oh no!" Roy realized who the guards thought was attacking the party. "Stay here!"

Roy didn't waste time running and used his magic to teleport to the location of the royal guards. What he saw proved his fear correct. Cal and Ceph were squaring off with the Candemon. They both were holding tridents and pointing them at the candy monster.

"Stay back, fiend!" one of the twins shouted.

"You are not going to crash our Princess's party!" said the other.

The Candemon's hard-candy eyes swiveled back and forth between the two guards. His mouth curved into a crooked line. "I was invited," he cried.

"Yeah, right. Who would invite an ugly monster to Polipo's Sweet Sixteen party? Get him, Cal!"

"You got it, Ceph."

How To Create A Villain

The two octonoids charged toward the Candemon, who lifted his candy-cane arms in defense. Roy immediately cast a rainbow between the two sides, causing Cal and Ceph to crash into it and collapse.

The Candemon turned to Roy. "What is this all about, Roy? You invite me then send guards after me? What cruel trick is this?"

"No, it isn't like that Candemon. I didn't have a chance to tell them you were coming yet." He helped the octonoids to their feet but made sure to keep the rainbow barrier between them and the Candemon. "Cal, Ceph: I invited him. He is here as my guest."

"Why would you invite such an ugly creature to Princess Polipo's birthday party?" asked one of the twins.

"Because," Roy answered, "He is part of Candy Island and deserves to be invited to the party." Roy walked through the rainbow barrier to stand beside the Candemon. "Why should he not be allowed just because of what he looks like?"

Cal kept a wary eye on the Candemon but addressed Roy. "It's not just that. It's the other thing . . . you know."

Roy waved his hand dismissively. "That's just a rumor. How do people know that his creator is dead anyway?"

Ceph replied, "Everyone knows, Roy. That creature shouldn't even exist in the Tooniverse anymore. He's stayed alive with some sort of trickery or evil."

"Everyone knows," Cal echoed.

"Well, I don't know," Roy said. "And on my Candy Island, you will not attack my guests. Put down your weapons so I can lower the barrier."

The guards angrily stabbed their tridents into the Rainbow PEZ road, sending bits of the rectangle candy flying into the grass to either side. "Fine," said Cal, "but you have to explain this one to the Princess."

Roy smiled. "I will." The guards picked up their tridents and scuttled away. Roy waved his hand to lower the rainbow barrier and stood face to gummy bear with the Candemon again.

"I think I should go," the Candemon said. "This was a bad idea, Roy."

"No, it isn't. I promise it will be okay. I'll protect you and make sure you are welcome. Do you trust me?"

The Candemon stood silent and motionless for a moment. Roy could feel the hard candy eyes trying to stare through him. He never let his smile falter, even though he felt quite uncomfortable. "I trust you, little gnome. And it better not be mislaid trust."

"Yay!" Roy cried. "Stay here. I'll go talk to the Princess and her guests to make sure they know you're coming. It's been crazy with all of the preparations and you came sooner than I expected. It'll be okay."

How To Create A Villain

Roy turned on the spot and ran back to the center of Taffy Towers where the party was to take place. Judging by the look on Princess Polipo's face, someone had already told her who her special guest was. "Roy! HOW COULD YOU?!" Roy reeled from the screech. He knew sirens that wish they could wail like that.

"Princess, he is your special guest. I thought you'd be happy."

"Happy to have that hideous monster ruin my party? Everyone else is trying to ruin it already. And now you, too? It is disgusting. My party is supposed to be beautiful and perfect!"

"And one of a kind, right?" Roy immediately saw that he had struck a chord with the princess. Her mouth curled into a smirk of entitlement. As spoiled as she was, Roy knew that Princess Polipo was not unintelligent. "A party like none of your friends from school have ever or will ever have. A party that people will talk about for years to come?"

The princess's smirk moved into a full-blown smile. The first smile Roy had seen on her all day. "You're right. No one has ever had a pet monster to perform for their party. Especially one as gross as the Candemon. I have to tell Jessica. She is going to be so jealous!" The princess ran away before Roy could correct her about the Candemon's status at the party.

"What could go wrong?" Roy thought to himself. "At least she won't have the guards attack him. . ."

* * *

Roy walked through the party that was going at full steam. He spied Princess Polipo talking to a very strong-looking pair of teenage mermen wearing UCHS letter jackets. He assumed they were members of the school's underwater football team. The princess seemed to be enjoying herself.

In a corner of the party, he found the Candemon sitting by himself holding a very tiny cup of punch. Roy could never read emotions on the Candemon's face, but he looked both sad and comical at the same time. Roy approached the Candemon and said, "How are you enjoying the party?"

"No one has tried to stab me with a trident in the last hour or so."

Roy chuckled, thinking the Candemon was being sarcastic. The lack of response from the Candemon made him wonder if that was the case. "Well, that's progress, right?"

"I still don't understand why I'm here, Roy. All this happiness around me only makes my isolation hurt more. Why are you trying to hurt me, gnome?"

"I am not trying to hurt you. I want you to be part of the joy. I want you to be happy like the rest of my Candy Island citizens."

How To Create A Villain

The Candemon made a motion that Roy thought was a shrug. It was hard to tell. "I am only a citizen here because that's where they sent me when I was sorted in Sorting Square all those years ago, Roy. I could just as well belong in Gothicville with the rest of the monsters."

"I have never known the sorters to get a location wrong, Candemon. And I've been here a long, long time. You belong here. Both on Candy Island and at this party. Come, let's go dance!" Roy took one of the Candemon's candy-cane arms and brought the monster to his feet. The Candemon's eyes grew a little wider, obviously startled by Roy's strength.

As Roy led the Candemon to the dance floor in front of Princess Polipo's stage, the crowd parted to make way. The music stopped abruptly as they reached the center of the floor and all around them fell silent. Roy ignored the stares and whisperings and began dancing.

"There's no music, Roy."

"There's always music in my head," Roy said. He then removed his hat and a very fast-paced jig echoed inside Taffy Towers, bouncing off the tall, colorful walls and filling the room with upbeat dance music. Roy encouraged the Candemon to dance by holding his candy-cane arms and shaking them back and forth the way one would do with a toddler at a wedding.

Roy was so engrossed in trying to help the Candemon fit in he didn't notice one of Princess Polipo's football player friends moving in behind the Candemon until it was too late. Roy went to shout at him, but was pushed out of the way as the other merman teen charged into the Candemon's gummy bear stomach.

"No!" Roy cried. But it was too late. The Candemon's unstable chocolate bar legs were already off balance and the monster tumbled backwards over the bent-over mer-teen.

CRASH!

The Candemon fell headfirst into the large ice cream sculpture of Princess Polipo and destroyed the entire centerpiece. He was covered in ice cream and various toppings and struggled to get to his feet.

Roy flew to his side. "Candemon? Are you okay?" He turned to the princess, now standing in the center of the dance floor with her face turning red from laughter. Roy could tell the boys committed the prank at her request. "Why would you do this, Princess? He is your guest!"

"No, Roy," she said. "He's your guest. He is *my* entertainment. Like you said, people will talk about this party for years. The party where the Candemon finally got put in his place." The hatred in Princess Polipo's voice gave Roy a pain in his chest.

How To Create A Villain

The Candemon finished flailing in the mess of ice cream, toppings, and shattered table to find his footing. He slowly stood and the ice cream fell from his candy apple head to the ground. He was shaking. Roy couldn't tell if it was from embarrassment or anger. Probably both, Roy wagered.

The Candemon spoke, his voice surprisingly calm and flat. "So this is why I was invited. I see now, Roy. I see why I was brought here." The Candemon's voice did not match his body language. He was still shaking. The stomach of the upside-down gummy-bear was beginning to have a golden glow.

"What is that?" asked Roy. "Why are you glowing? I hear a sound." Roy took a step away from the Candemon as the golden glow grew stronger. He could hear a voice slowly starting to grow from the Candemon's chest.

"Help me," a faint female voice cried. "Help me out of here."

"O M G," cried the gathered teens from Underwater City and various guests from Candy Island. "It's true!"

"SHUT UP ELEANOR!" the Candemon screamed, silencing the murmuring of the crowd. "Silence!" The golden glow immediately dulled to a very small spark, barely noticeable unless one looked closely.

"So the rumors are true, then." Roy let his smile fade away. It actually hurt his face to not be smiling, he found. "That spark. That glow is . . . your creator's essence? You captured her essence when she died so you could live on?"

The Candemon's face contorted into a twisted smile. "Not all of us get to live forever like you, Roy. We aren't all Originals. But I do get to live forever. As long as Eleanor doesn't die, I live. Don't you see?"

"That is awful!" cried Polipo. "You really are a monster, inside and out!"

"I'm no more a monster than you, Princess Polipo. I just accept what I am. And since you and Roy plotted so well to get me to this party to 'entertain' you all, how about a demonstration?"

Roy stood motionless as the Candemon shook the remaining debris from his body and roared. He spat molten marshmallow at the crowd and encased half the crowd in a white prison. He charged at the two football players and knocked them into the air. "Batter up!" he cried as he swung his arms like a bat, propelling the strong mer-teens into the stage, bringing the entire setup to the ground in a heap.

Roy snapped out of his trance and shouted, "NO!" He raised a hand and instantly trapped the Candemon inside a rainbow ball. The monster smashed at the ball but couldn't break it. His widened eyes showed shock at Roy's power. "Stop," Roy mumbled.

How To Create A Villain

"But isn't this what you wanted, Roy? Isn't this why I'm here? Let me continue giving this little brat her unforgettable party." He pointed an arm at Princess Polipo, who was cowering next to the rubble of her Sweet Sixteen stage. "Let me continue to entertain her. She looks entertained, does she not?"

"Stop it, Candemon."

"You're the one who brought me here. This is your fault, Roy."

Roy raised his hand to the sky, causing the Candemon-filled rainbow ball to also rise. "You're wrong Candemon. Everything about you is wrong. You still existing is wrong. I knew the rumors. I thought that, even if they were true, you could coexist with other creations. How different were you, after all?"

"More different than you could imagine, Roy G. Biv. I'm immortal. I'm closer to you Originals than these fleeting creation toons you love so much."

"No you are not. Go home, Candemon. You were right. You don't belong here." Roy flicked his wrist and flung the Candemon's ball out of Taffy Towers and into the horizon. The monster's screams slowly faded as the ball hurtled away from the destroyed party.

Roy could hear him calling, "I'll be baaaaack."

"Are you happy, Roy?" Polipo cried from the wreck. "You ruined my party. Why would you invite that monster?"

"No, Polipo, you ruined your party. You and your friends being unwilling to accept someone who looked different and had a different background than you. You brought this upon your own party."

Polipo bent down to stare Roy in the eyes. "But you saw it, Roy. You heard him admit that he was an Anomaly. You even said yourself that him existing is wrong."

Roy plopped on the ground and let out a long exhale. "But it isn't our place to right that wrong, Polipo. He shouldn't exist but he does. Better to just let him alone. The Tooniverse will right the wrong in time. It always does."

"But . . . what about my party?"

Roy looked around at the destruction, including half the crowd mumbling from encasements of solidified marshmallow. "It will be remembered for years to come, as you wished. Especially by the Candemon. Whatever happens in the future, just remember your role in creating your own enemy, Princess. He was content being left alone. It was you and I who pushed him, figuratively and literally."

"But what could he possibly do to you us, Roy? He is no match for your power."

"Let's hope we never find out." Roy stood and swept debris with his foot. "Now let's clean up. I think your party is over."

The Grave Little Toaster

Author Note:

When I first started writing this story, I wasn't entirely sure I considerd it a "Toonopolis" story. It certainly matches the humorous tone. In retrospect, I consider this a new section of Toonopolis (Suburbia!) that does not, at time of print, appear in any other Toonopolis story. I was heavily inspired by the TV series *Santa Clarita Diet* in writing this stort story and anyone who watched that show will see the parallels in the "paranormal activity starring bumbling suburbanites" concept.

It was first published in *Demonic Household*, the second volume of Battle Goddess Productions' *Demonic Anthology* series in August 2018. It was edited by Valerie Willis.

"hy do you call?" cried the disembodied and hollow voice in the darkness.

"Oh my god, Janet, the spell is working! What have we done?" a male voice called.

"Shut up, Brad," Janet snapped. "Get the vessel."

A swirling vortex of red and purple smoke began forming in the air. The pitch-blackness of the unlit room highlighted the oddity of smoke that emanated its own light. The red portion of the smoke became centralized and formed something approximate to eyes on the shapeless purple form.

"Brad!" Janet cried. "We need the vessel!"

The smoke's 'eyes' narrowed as it scanned the room. Even though it cast its own minute light, there was nothing to see in the dark. It tilted the top of its plume to the side, as though it were listening.

"I form!" the smoke-creature bellowed. "I shall feast on your souls, amateurs," it added with a snicker. "You know not with what you meddle. Do you know who I am?"

"I got it," Brad called.

"Are you sure?" Janet asked.

Brad sighed. "Must you question everything I do, Janet? This is carving the turkey on Thanksgiving all over again. I'm not an idiot, darling."

"You absolutely destroyed that turkey, honey," she replied.

The Grave Little Toaster

"Are you two done?" the creature asked. The vortex slowed and was beginning to form the shape of something almost human. Judging by the amount of smoke left, the creature would tower over eight-feet tall when it was done amalgamating itself.

"Put it in the circle," Janet commanded.

"Yes, dear," Brad complied.

"I hunger for your souls!" the summoned smoke demon mocked. "Please enter the circle, Brad."

There was a rustling of sound to the smoke monster's left and its red eyes scanned the darkness for what it presumed to be the male human responsible for its summoning. A clanging sound rung out below the smoke and the demon looked down. A metallic object had been tossed into the circle. These humans were smarter than they looked. They had a vessel prepared to contain him. Hopefully they won't know the way to bind—

"I command you, Mephistocrates the Hungerer, to enter this vessel until I release you from your prison or you complete my request," Janet said in a cadence that suggested she was reciting a memorized line.

Mephistocrates felt itself bound the second she used its name. How did this obviously weak practitioner know the name of such an ancient and powerful demon? The demon bounced around the circle and felt no weaknesses in the implementation of the power. It was flawless.

"Do you hear me, demon?" Janet beckoned.

It stopped struggling. Mephistocrates was bound and knew it. Best to just get this over with. The demon allowed itself to be sucked into the vessel that was thrown into the circle and stopped fighting. "What do you request?" it asked.

"I told you it would work, Brad," Janet mocked.

"I didn't say it wouldn't, honey. I just was a little worried that summoning a demon based on instructions from a Reddit forum would be disappointing or dangerous."

"Well, my great-great-great-great grandmother was burned as a witch in Salem, you know. It's in my blood."

"What do you request?" Mephistocrates repeated. It was hoping to get this over with so it no longer had to listen to Brad and Janet bickering.

Janet took a breath in the darkness and commanded, "I wish for you to end the lives of Chris and Karen Smythe, our neighbors across the street."

"I shall do as you command," the demon answered. "What slight have these Smythes borne upon you that they require such a final judgment?"

Brad sighed.

"There have been many and sundry slights," Janet began in her best formal voice to match the demon's. "The time Karen bought the same bathing suit as me after she definitely saw me buying it at the mall. The way Chris mows his lawn at seven o'clock in the morning on Saturdays."

"He still has my hedge clippers," Brad added.

"Yes, that too. But the final straw was when they clearly cheated to win the homeowner's association's annual gardening competition that Brad and I have won every year for the last twelve years. Bribing the judge with brownies. Who does that?"

There was silence as Mephistocrates processed the information given to it by the couple that summoned it. "Are these grievances so egregious as to justify death?" the demon ventured.

"Absolutely," Janet said with a scoff. "Now do as I command, demon!"

The shrill pitch of Janet's voice hurt Mephistocrates. There was power in her words but the demon couldn't tell if it was the supposed witch's blood in her veins or the underlying expectation that this woman would clearly get what she wanted via persistence even without it.

"I accept your charge, m'lady," the demon answered. "I shall be bound to you until such time as you release me or I complete your request. You may return light to the world and break my circle. You have my word that I shall commit you no harm."

A flicked switch turned on overhead lighting and the basement of a house came into view. Mephistocrates looked around from its vessel on the concrete floor of the building. A space had been cleared in the center of the room and, as the demon realized, a perfectly executed circle of power was drawn on the stone in chalk. It looked up at the two humans that had summoned it and saw nothing special. They had yellow hair and appeared fairly average in practically all things humans used to measure one another.

"Jesus, Brad, what did you do?" Janet asked.

"I thought it was the vessel. It was dark!" Brad answered, terrified of the woman's calm tone. "Can't we just transfer it to the right one?"

"It's not a damn MP3, you idiot! There were no instructions other than letting it complete its task from within the vessel. Anything short of that is opening us up to letting Mephistocrates take control of the situation. That is why they said to put him into something with limbs it can control!" Janet slapped Brad across the back of his head and muttered to herself. She walked away from him and picked up a small metal soldier, which about a foot tall and wielding serious, if tiny, weapons. "How did you confuse that—" She pointed to the demon at the center of the circle. "—With this?" she held up the soldier.

"They're both metal?" Brad asked.

The Grave Little Toaster

"If I could intrude," Mephistocrates said politely from the floor, "could I ask what vessel I have been contained in?"

Janet threw the soldier at Brad, who cowered and received the blow. "Let me show you what this moron did," she said to the demon. She retrieved a small circular mirror and placed it in front of Mephistocrates and let the demon gaze into it.

In the reflective surface, Mephistocrates observed a rectangular metal object. It was approximately the size of the soldier but had no arms or legs. The demon hopped around to get a look at the side of its vessel and saw a few knobs and a lever. A long tail protruded from one end and the demon swung it around to see two small metal prongs poking out from a molded plastic. "What is this device?" it asked.

"It's a toaster. You're in a damn toaster," Janet sighed.

* * *

"That was a lovely service," she said.

"Still hard to believe they're dead," he replied. "I still have Brad's hedge clippers you know. How does that work? Are they mine now?"

"That's terrible, Chris. You shouldn't joke about things like that."

Mephistocrates, from its perch on the kitchen counter where he had been resting, watched Chris and Karen Smythe enter the room in their best funeral clothes. It had been stewing and biding its time since the "toaster" was gifted to the Smythes as a good will gesture several weeks ago. Or had it been months? For an eternal being, human constructs of time were hard to follow. The demon was banking on simply not completing the request in the hopes that it could convince Janet to release it eventually. It wasn't that Mephistocrates had a problem with killing humans who didn't really seem to deserve it. He just didn't really feel like it.

But now he had to.

When it heard that Janet and Brad had died in a car crash, the demon's plan for getting released fell through. Now Mephistocrates had only once course of action: complete the dead woman's command and thus be free from the bindings of the ritual spell that kept it on this plane of existence.

"If you want my opinion," Chris continued, "Brad drove off that bridge on purpose. I bet he felt death was better than listening to Janet call him an idiot or talk about how everything he did was always wrong." Chris mimicked driving a car and sharply turned the imaginary wheel to the right, making screeching sounds. "Game over."

"I didn't ask for your opinion, dear," Karen said through a smile. "It doesn't change the fact that two people are dead right now. I still think it's wrong to make fun of the dead. What if they haunt us?" She sad down at the table next to her husband and took his hand. "I know you don't believe in those things, but I do. We weren't on great terms in life. I'd hate to have them as enemies in the afterlife too."

Chris squeezed Karen's hand. "I'm sorry. You're right. Would now be a bad time to ask about that?" He pointed to the toaster on the counter.

"The toaster? Why?"

Chris rose from the table and ran fingers through his dark hair. "Isn't it a little weird to keep it now? I know the Hendersons gave it to us as a 'sorry we got angry about the gardening contests' gift but why would they give us an old toaster as a gift? It's just kind of . . . weird," he repeated.

"What would you suggest we do with it?"

"Throw it in the trash? We don't even use it." Chris pointed to the superior toaster oven in black and chrome that sat to the left of the demonically possessed toaster. "It's only out there because you were afraid Janet would ask why we weren't using it if they stopped by."

"But..."

Chris held up his hand. "I know, I know. Ghosts. What's the statute of limitations on keeping a useless gift from a dead person? A month? Two?"

Mephistocrates listened to the conversation in earnest. Many a demon has been in this situation before. Getting trapped in some sort of vessel for an indeterminate time is one of the most infamous ways for a demon to go missing from their plane for millennia. It would be damn sure to not add its name to the tales of warning told to freshly spawned demonic entities. Toaster limitations aside, it was time to act.

That evening while the Smythes slept, Mephistocrates began its plan. The first step would require an elimination of the demon's shelfmate and competition for bread-warming option. The demon used its tail that the humans hadn't even bothered to plug in to slowly sever the tail of the fancier toaster oven beside it on the counter. "And now," it thought, "we wait."

* * *

"What on earth did this?" Karen asked the next morning. She was holding the severed cord of the shiny toaster oven in the air so Chris could see.

Chris looked behind the oven and saw the cleanly cut cord still plugged into the wall. "It looks like it was cut with a knife. That is so strange." He reached to unplug the remaining cord from the wall.

Mephistocrates grinned, to the extent that it could grin without a mouth.

"Wait," Karen called.

Chris pulled his hand away from the cord. "I don't know what I was thinking. Thanks. I'll shut the breaker first." He exited the kitchen into an adjacent room. After a few moments, he returned, unplugged the cut end of the cord, and removed the now-broken toaster oven from the shelf. "Guess we'll have to get a new one," he mused as he exited the room again.

"I still need to toast this bagel," Karen said. "Flip the breaker back on and I'll just use this one," she called to Chris in the other room. The female human slide the less fancy toaster over and plugged it into the vacated socket.

Mephistocrates felt the surge in power as the circuit was opened and electricity flowed into its vessel. The demon was not put off by the lack of success in the male human not electrocuting himself stupidly. It was a simple tactic but was worth a try. "Now to test the female," it mused.

Karen dropped two circular pieces of bread into the open slots on the toaster and pressed down on the lever.

As she moved around the kitchen, making coffee and obtaining some sort of cheese from the refrigerator, Mephistocrates watched and waited. It could feel the electricity convert into heat within its metal coils and the bagel slowly cooked. When the internal mechanism that served for a timer, the demon allowed the heat to stop but held firm onto the bagel halves with its walls.

"This thing should be done by now," Karen said as she returned to the counter. She looked down inside the toaster and sighed. "Oh great, it's stuck." She pushed up on the lever in an attempt to release the toasted bagel but it didn't budge.

"What's wrong?" Chris asked.

"The stupid bagel is stuck. Of course Janet would give me a busted toaster as an apology gift."

"Can I throw it out yet?" The silence as Karen fiddled with the lever more lingered and Chris didn't pursue the line of questioning any further.

Karen opened a nearby drawer and shuffled around with utensils. She obtained one and slammed the door shut. "I'm already late for work and if I don't eat I will not be happy," she said more to the toaster than Chris.

Mephistocrates sat patiently waiting. All she had to do was use that utensil to try to get the bagel out and the demon could send a jolt of electricity through her to stop her heart. Crude but effective. It felt the utensil make contact with its metal coils and released the stored electricity.

And nothing happened.

Karen cried triumphantly as she released first one half of the bagel and then the other with a plastic fork. "I'll order a new toaster oven today," she told Chris while smearing butter on her bagel. "You can throw it out when we have the new one."

The demon fumed inside its useless vessel and plotted its next move. It could no longer think like a being with infinite time. It had a deadline now: kill the humans before its 'replacement' arrived or be doomed to potential eons in this vessel.

While Karen and Chris left the house unattended to do whatever it is humans do all day, Mephistocrates prepared for its next move. It used its control over the object to hop off the counter and explore the domicile, a two-story building far larger than the two of them needed for just themselves. The demon considered the irony of its massive form being trapped inside such a small vessel while they moved around freely in this structure. Even if they didn't deserve death for their supposed affronts to Janet and Brad, Mephistocrates felt this injustice alone was worthy of the sentence.

The possessed toaster slowly made its way upstairs to the second floor and there the demon set in motion its next plan. In its observation, a good fall from such a height was more than enough to eliminate a human. They were a fragile bunch.

Mephistocrates sat at the top of the stairs and plotted. It whipped its tail around the uppermost railing and pulled it taut across the landing. Once again, crude, but the demon had no other choices with its limited vessel. It didn't even have limbs. It disconnected the cord and found a closet near the stairs in which to wait until morning.

* * *

CRASH! BANG! CRUNCH!

"Oh my God, Chris, are you okay?" Karen screamed from atop the stairs.

Chris lay in a heap at the bottom of the stairs. The door to the coat closet was broken in two pieces on top of him. There was no movement.

"Chris?" Karen quested again. She stepped gingerly over the electrical cord slung across the top stair and ran to the bottom. As she got there, the pile of wood that used to be a door moved and Chris emerged from the debris.

"I'm okay," he said. He was bleeding from a few places but was otherwise steady on his feet. "What did I trip over?"

The two humans both looked up at the toaster sitting on the side of the top step with its cord tied across to the railing and shivered.

Karen spoke first. "Who would have put that there?"

Chris brushed off some splinters of wood from his pajama pants and winced. He rotated his shoulder suggesting some sort of injury. "Well, if it wasn't you with some elaborate prank, I certainly wouldn't have tripped myself with it!"

Karen walked back up the stairs and untied the cord. Picking up the toaster, she said, "I think it's time we get rid of this thing. I am totally freaked out by it now."

The Grave Little Toaster

"If I had known falling down some stairs would have gotten you to see my side of this, I would have done it days ago," Chris said with a laugh.

"Wait!" the disembodied voice inside the toaster shouted.

Karen dropped the toaster and it rolled down the stairs and directly into Chris's crotch.

"Ugh!" he called, doubling over in additional pain.

"I'm so sorry!" she said, running back down the stairs. "It talked!"

Chris lifted the toaster and looked it over. "It talked?"

"Yes," the voice said again.

Chris avoided dropping it but held it a little further away from his body. He stepped out of the broken door pieces and walked to the living room, placing the toaster down on the coffee table along the way.

Karen followed. "Is it the ghost of the Hendersons?"

"Like one shared ghost or both of them in the toaster?" Chris asked. He sat down with a groan and wiped some blood from his forehead.

"I don't know. But what the hell?" she asked.

"Good question." Chris turned his attention to the toaster. "So what the hell?"

"I am not a ghost. Or several ghosts," Mephistocrates explained from within his vessel. "I am a demon summoned by your Hendersons to dispatch with you due to their jealousy over losing some type of contest."

Karen let out a breath of air covered in anger. "That bitch summoned a demon over an HOA gardening competition with a fifty dollar gift card to Applebee's?"

"So it would seem," the demon added.

"What the hell is wrong with her?" Karen asked rhetorically.

"Aside from being dead?" the toaster asked.

Chris laughed. "I like this guy. Hey, did you kill our toaster oven?"

"I had to try to complete my objective," the demon explained. "I am bound by my charge to kill you in order to be released back to my plane of existence. As the Hendersons are now dead, there is no other way for me to escape this vessel."

"Man, that sucks," Chris said.

"I can't believe you are sympathizing with the demon that is trying to kill us," Karen cried. "And also broke our toaster oven," she added after a thought. She drew her attention to the mess of broken door at the bottom of the stairs and pointed emphatically to it. "Also that."

"Oh come on," Chris said. "He didn't ask to be summoned here. You shouldn't be mad at him. Janet and Brad are to blame. And I don't even blame Brad that much. I still think he crashed on purpose to get away from her."

"I surmise you are correct, Chris," Mephistocrates said. "It is his fault I am stuck in this inadequate vessel but she was the one that summoned me."

"That guy really couldn't do anything right," Karen said.

"Don't start," Chris said.

There was an awkward moment of silence as the three of them sat staring at one another. Mephistocrates broke the silence with a question, "So now what?" it asked.

"How come you're allowed to talk to us?" Chris asked. "Like shouldn't your presence be a secret or something?"

"Not a rule, per se," the demon answered. "Usually better to have the element of surprise but I had to change my plan when I realized you would simply discard me to exist in this vessel alone for demons know how long. Originally, I attempted to reason with the one you call Janet."

"You cannot reason with that woman," Karen said.

"So I discovered," Mephistocrates said. "Then I attempted, feebly I may add, to still complete her command. And now, I attempt to reason with you."

Chris rubbed his shoulder. "You couldn't have tried that before tripping me down the stairs?"

"It's generally far easier to kill someone than it is to reason with them," it said.

"Hard to argue with that logic," Chris assented.

"What exactly are we discussing here?" Karen asked.

"Just trying to figure out the rules and limitations. What harm could there be?" Chris turned his attention back to the toaster. "So you're like a demon and not a genie or anything, right?"

Mephistocrates pondered the question. "That depends on perspective, really. I am of a different plane of existence than you, much like all spirit beings. I do not grant wishes, however, so don't bother asking."

"So what's your deal, then? You harvest souls for Satan?"

The laughter was tinny coming from the toaster but it rang out heartily. "Of course not. That fool. I feast on souls." Mephistocrates paused as the humans, especially the female one, shivered. It debated whether or not to continue but figured there were worse options. "I am called Mephistocrates the Hungerer."

"I think I'll call you Mitchell," Chris said.

The Grave Little Toaster

"What?" both Karen and Mephistocrates said at the same time.

Karen stared incredulously at her husband. "You can't be seriously thinking about keeping him around? He may try to kill us again."

"Maybe," Chris said. "But what if we come up with a new deal, Mitch."

The toaster turned to the side as though it were thinking. "I'm listening."

"You're stuck there until we die, right?"

"Until I kill you," the demon corrected.

"Okay, fine," Chris accepted. "Until you kill us. But you're like an eternal demon, right? We've only got a good fifty to sixty years left in the tank. That's nothing to someone like you, isn't it?"

"I suppose."

"So you stay with us. Make sure we stay protected and alive and, when the time comes, we'll make sure you get credit for our deaths. It's either that or we can toss you in the trash and you end up on the bottom of a landfill forever."

Karen's mouth dropped open. She stared back and forth from her husband to the toaster. She didn't say anything, however.

Mephistocrates thought about the offer. This human was beyond reasonable. In fact, he was pretty smart. He found a way to benefit himself within the initial parameters of the summoner's charge and the demon would only need to wait a single human lifespan. This deal was too good to pass up. And, if an opportunity arrived, Mephistocrates could always just kill them along the way when their guard was down.

"You have yourself a deal," the toaster said.

"Welcome to the family, Mitch! I think we're gonna be good friends," Chris said with a smile.

Misanthrope Beechworth & The Dustwaste Wellspring

Author Note:

This novella has quite an interesting story behind it. I originally intended for Missy's tale to be a short story to submit to a Sci-Fi anthology of teen heroines who were involved in STEM fields. After introducing her in *Toonopolis: Chi Lin*, I thought her backstory would be fun. After about a third of the way through the story, I realized it was going to be a much longer tale (and had to submit a cyberpunk story to the aforementioned anthology instead). The result: Missy's tale was able to go as long as it needed and very well may set the stage for a dedicated steampunk series starring her!

It was original published in eBook only in January 2019 by Portmanteau Press LLC. Like the Anchihiiroo novella, this is the first time this story is available in print. It was edited by Jessica West.

Part One: The Toymaker's Daughter

Misanthrope Beechworth looked at the pile of bills on her father's workbench and sighed. Scattered on top of tools, springs, gears, and bits of metal were notices from Steamport Power Company, Metallurgist Winthrop—who supplied her father with the metals he used to craft his wonderful toys—and Baron von Deutsch, their landlord. At least two of them read *Final Notice* in bold red type across the front.

"Don't you worry yourself over adult problems, Missy," her father calmly said from behind her. "It'll be okay."

Missy peered again at the past-due notifications then turned to face her father. Simon Beechworth was not a large man. As it was, Missy nearly came eye-to-eye with the toymaker, even though she was barely five feet tall herself and only fifteen years old. She lowered her eyes from his when she saw the pain hiding behind his ever-present smile. Her hands instinctively touched the goggles she always wore around her neck, and fidgeted with them.

"We've been in financial trouble before, Misa."

She cringed at the nickname only her dad used for her. The one he only used when he still thought of her as a baby. She wasn't feeling it today.

"Maybe if you charged more than barely above cost for the toys the noble kids seem to love so much." Missy gestured to the shelves around the workshop littered with various in-production wind-up and tinker toys. "And didn't give them away to the scavenger kids," she mumbled.

Her father sighed. "Misa—"

"It's Missy, father. I'm not a little kid anymore."

The petite tinkerer sighed again. "I know. I know." He held up his hands in defeat. "I will consider your advice," he added.

Missy only heard a small amount of condescension in his voice, so she took it as a win. Her father wasn't a bad guy, not even close; but sometimes he struggled to accept that his little girl was basically an adult by Steamport standards, especially in Scraptown. Fifteen-year-old nobles still went to school and played games in The Reach—the upper portions of Steamport's sprawling, haphazardly constructed metropolis, where the air was cleaner and the streets were wider. Fifteen-year-old Scraptown kids, though? They went to work.

She glanced over her shoulder at the table one last time. Missy knew her father had gotten out of similar trouble in the past, but it seemed exceptionally bad this time. She also knew she wasn't going to win this argument.

Simon Beechworth would never change his motto of "people over profits," and he'd rather go without than see an unhappy child in Scraptown. Even if it meant adopting a stubborn little girl when her mother died ten years ago.

Missy bent over and picked up her leather satchel and slung it over her shoulder. A metallic clang rang as an object fell from the bag and struck the wooden planks of the floor.

Her father reached down and retrieved the item. He beamed a genuine smile as he looked at it. "Sprocket," he almost whispered. "You still carry him around with you?"

Missy's cheeks grew warm. Sprocket was a toy cat her father made for her just after the adoption, when she was just five years old. He was one-of-a-kind, with shiny titanium gears at the joints of his limbs contrasting with his copper body in a beautiful metallic two-tone appearance. The toy had been modified only once since her father built him. Missy's childhood friend from Animetown replaced the cat's original glass eyes with green LED lights that were wired to his battery and gave Sprocket a unique, almost-sentient look. He was special in so many ways.

The toymaker held the cat out to Missy, who took him and stuffed him back into her bag.

"I'm late to meet Rube, father. We gotta get to work." She gave her father a quick hug and slid the metal door to the workshop—which was also their home—to the side.

"Be safe out there, Misa," her father said, slipping in the epithet one more time.

"I will, papa," she said without correcting him. Missy pushed the door closed behind her and stepped into the busy and claustrophobic Scraptown street where their shop stood. She looked up at the almost plain-looking sign hanging above the door. Basic script in white paint on a piece of scrap copper read *Beechworth Toys.* "Maybe we need a better sign," she said to no one in particular.

Missy looked past the sign at the giant clock tower that stood in the central square of Scraptown. "Frick," she cursed, seeing that she only had thirty minutes to collect Rube and meet with the dockmaster or she'd lose pay. She glanced up at the plain, old sign again. She could not afford to have her pay docked.

She adjusted her backpack, touched her goggles, and broke into a run through the crowded street toward the clock tower. Her small frame let her weave in and out of the crowd like an old-school motorcycle moved through traffic back when roads still connected the cities. She received a few "hey" and "watch it" calls along the way, but made it to the tower in near record time.

Misanthrope Beechworth & The Dustwaste Wellspring

All the major streets of Scraptown ended—or began, depending on perspective—at the square. They spanned straight out from the clock tower in eight cardinal directions like spokes in a wheel. Beechworth Toys was on Southeast Way. Her best friend Rube Silverburg lived with his parents on North Way, so she had to cut straight through the square to get to his house.

She stopped when she hit the square, though. A huge crowd gathered at the base of the clock tower blocked her path. A fancy-dressed man stood on a raised dais at the base of the square. Missy recognized him at once by the mechanical brass rose pinned to his black overcoat. Throw in the golden monocle, silk top hat, and perfectly groomed handlebar mustache, and Lord Benson Fearing was unmistakable. Everyone knew Lord Benson, the head of the Royal Order of Scavengers and Engineers. ROSE practically ran Steamport. Even the nobles in The Reach respected inducted members of ROSE.

"And today, ladies and gentlemen of Steamport," Lord Benson said through a handheld amplifier, "we give you that chance! Best of luck to you all!"

With a flourish, Lord Benson picked up what looked like a rocket launcher from the ground at his feet and fired it into the air. Confetti the size of full sheets of paper rained into the square and the crowd scrambled to retrieve them. Missy raised an eyebrow at the fervor of the crowd. She'd clearly missed the big announcement, only catching the end of Lord Fearing's speech. She waited for the pages to fall to the ground and snatched up one of them. It was a flyer with an embossed brass rose emblazoned in the center.

"Come one, come all," Missy read from the flyer. "The Royal Order of Scavengers and Engineers invites all participants to join our first annual Inventionfest Open. Prizes awarded for new and original inventions, including a grand prize of ten thousand bits."

Missy picked up her jaw from the floor and understood why the crowd was going insane. Almost everyone in Scraptown was a tinkerer or inventor of some sort. It wasn't that they were all engineering geniuses or anything, it was just that when you lived in a place called Scraptown, you learned to use what you had to get by, whether it was retrofitting an old hot water heater into a bathtub or hammering some scrap metal into a cup. She looked at Lord Fearing, who was smiling and waving to the crowd, and then up at the clock tower again.

"Frick," she swore again. Missy shoved the flyer into her satchel and tore through the crowd to make her way to Rube's house.

Part Two: The Scavengers' Son

When she arrived at the Silverburgs' home, Missy was out of breath. Rube's parents were scavengers who were the children of scavengers who were also the children of scavengers. As it stood, they had prime real estate on North Way. Missy banged on the metal plate that served as their door. No one answered. She banged again. Still no answer.

"Pull the lever!" called a voice from the other side of the door.

Missy sighed and looked at the lever attached to the wall to the right of the door. Sure enough, there was a note dangling from it that read *Pull Me*. She did as the note commanded. Pulling the lever revealed a string attached to it.

"Great," she mumbled. "Another one of Rube's inventions."

Rube Silverburg, as reliable and fun as he had been throughout their childhood, had a tendency to waste a lot of time with useless inventions. Entertaining and clever, perhaps, but they were still generally useless. Missy followed the string with her eyes and saw that it pulled down a piece of wood that was slotted inside a tube. As the wood moved, a small marble rolled down the tube. It struck a larger marble on the end and sent it rolling as well. The larger marble fell into a cup, which raised a lever into a row of wooden dominoes. The dominoes toppled one another until the final one struck a tin bell that let out a very faint *ding*. Missy waited a moment to see if anything else would happen. It didn't.

The door to the house slid open and Rube was standing there with a proud grin on his face. The grin only served to accentuate his poor attempt at growing facial hair and raised his thick glasses an inch or so above his nose so they didn't quite line up with his big brown eyes.

"And?" Missy said.

Rube's smile didn't waver. "It's my new doorbell. Do you like it?"

Missy looked up at the overly complicated contraption. "Why not just have the lever ring the bell? I mean, that would be simpler."

"You have no vision, Beechworth," Rube decried. "That would be boring."

"No," Missy said. "That would be practical."

"How is this not practical? It rang the bell, didn't it?"

Missy reached over and pulled the lever again. The slotted piece of wood moved out of the way of a now non-existent marble. Nothing happened beyond that. Missy held up her hands in a *see that* gesture.

"Well sure, if you want to ring the bell more than once. But who does that?"

"What if you don't hear it the first time? What if, I don't know, a second person is dumb enough to visit you in the same day? And don't you have to reset the marbles and dominoes after each time the bell is rung?" Missy pulled the lever again to further demonstrate its uselessness.

"You're no fun."

"Speaking of no fun, we're going to be late to the docks if you don't get out here and get moving."

"Fine," Rube conceded. He reached to the side and grabbed his work bag. "Let me just reset the doorbell before we go."

Missy reached through the doorway and punched him in the chest.

"Ow!" He rubbed at his chest. "Fine, I'll do it later." He turned his head to call back into the house. "Mom, Dad, I'm headed to work with Missy. Don't wait up!" He slung his bag over his shoulder and slid the door shut, then stepped back to admire the lever and his overly complicated doorbell setup. "You know, you might be right about that ringing the bell more than once problem."

Missy smacked him on the back of the head, which was hard because he was nearly a foot taller than her and she had to jump to do it. She felt it was worth the effort, though, because it made such a satisfying smacking sound that just didn't feel the same when she hit him in the back. "Let's get to work, you doofus."

"That's Mr. Doofus to you," he corrected.

Missy looked down North Way toward the clock tower and saw they only had ten minutes left to get to work on time. Thankfully, she thought, the docks were at the end of North Way opposite the square. This was where the Silverburgs' prime real estate came into play. The oldest scavenger families were closest to the docks. She nudged her head at the clock tower.

Rube followed her gaze and let out a whistle. "Guess we better get going."

"You think?"

"Race ya!" Rube said, breaking into a run toward the docks. His longer legs gave him a definite advantage over Missy when it came to speed, so he had a big head start.

Missy grumbled to herself and ran as well. Where Rube's height gave him a longer gait, Missy's size gave her more agility to not crash into people as she tore through the crowd. Overall, it was a fairly even race, considering the setting. Once again, random people in the crowd shouted and cursed at the teenagers as they ran.

The clock tower gave out eight sharp metallic rings just as Rube reached the back of the work line at the docks. Missy arrived half a step later and Rube looked down at her again with that dopey grin of his.

"You cheated," Missy declared while catching her breath.

"How is that?" Rube asked knowingly. "I didn't stop growing?"

"Stupid puberty," she spat. When they were younger, Missy was taller than her friend. Then came Mother Nature and her hormones and she understood why the older folk used the phrase "growing like a weed" when it came to pre-teen boys.

Rube patted Missy on the head, which was pretty much the worst thing a tall person could do to a short person. Of course, Rube knew this, so Missy shrugged it off so as not to give him the satisfaction of knowing she was annoyed.

Then she yanked his work bag off his shoulder and dropped it on the ground behind her. While Rube scrambled to recover it, she stepped in line in front of him just as Dockmaster Wharton was handing a timecard to the boy in front of her in line. She grabbed hers next and looked back at Rube. "I win," she said.

"And she says I'm the cheater," Rube grumbled as he retrieved his card from the burly dockmaster. He looked at his card and let out a whine.

"What's yer issue?" Dockmaster Wharton said through the long pipe he always had clenched in his teeth.

"Von Deutsch's crew? Why do we always get stuck with him?" Rube complained.

"Maybe you should get here on time. Or maybe even early," Wharton said with a half-grin.

Missy pulled Rube away from the large and tough-looking dockmaster before Rube could turn the grin into a snarl. She'd seen it happen enough times to know that it didn't take much. She held her timecard up to Rube. "Look, I got von Deutsch too. At least we'll work together today."

"More like von Douche," Rube muttered. He followed Missy to the punch machine and watched her slip her card in. The gears in the machine made a soft whirring sound as it marked the time they clocked into work. He slid his in then placed it on the pile next to the machine. "I just hope he doesn't put his son in charge of the crew again today."

Missy couldn't disagree with Rube on that point. As much of a stereotypical jerk of a noble as Baron Hans von Deutsch was, his son Heinrich was ten times worse. She said, "He's the biggest von Douche of them all."

Part Three: The Noble's Son

A haughty throat-clearing noise came from behind Missy and Rube.

Missy knew who it was before she even turned around. She did so anyway and plastered a huge smile on her face. "Heinrich! How are you doing today?"

Heinrich von Deutsch was even taller than Rube, but built like a machinist or blacksmith with large arms and shoulders. He had to be at least six-foot-four. He had piercing blue eyes and perfectly blond, short-cropped, military hair in ROSE Academy student style. He wore his academy uniform: a navy blue blazer over a white shirt with a gold tie. His crisp white slacks were perfectly pressed in what Missy presumed to be regulation pleats. Her eyes lingered on the embroidered brass rose on his sleeve and she recalled the flyer she'd had to quickly stuff into her satchel. She had to talk to Rube about it still.

"Miss Beechword," Heinrich said with a slight nasal tone.

Missy wondered how nobles always managed to have that same way of talking. Did they teach it or was it learned? Or was there some sort of genetic trait that gave them all deviated septums?

"It's Beechworth," she corrected politely but firmly.

The huge Academy student looked at Rube and continued, "Mister Silverburg."

Rube saluted.

Missy wasn't sure if he was being serious or mocking the bigger, older teenager. He was only two years older than Missy and Rube, but was one year from graduating ROSE Academy and being inducted as a full member of the order. He was practically royalty at this point. Between his father's money and connections and his own well-known ability as an engineer, Heinrich von Deutsch walked around like he was untouchable. Missy hated pretty much everything about him.

Heinrich walked past them and toward his father's ship on the dock, the skyship *Platinschiff*. The gangplank was down and he boarded without another word.

Missy and Rube fell in with a group of six other Scraptown folk who were assigned to the *Platinschiff* for work that day. They ranged in ages from twelve— when Scraptown kids left school and started working— to some in their twenties whose bodies could still hold up to the rigors of scavenging work. The silent shuffle of the workers was the eeriest part of the morning. Missy looked around and saw how miserable they all were and figured she was at least lucky to have Rube to keep her from falling down that pit of despair like many of the others did. Or maybe Rube was lucky to have her.

Heinrich stood on the pristine wooden dock of the ship and held his hands behind his back, pushing his enormously muscled chest forward. "Good morning, ladies and gentlemen. As you can tell, my father could not be here today so I will be supervising your work. Please bear in mind that this is no excuse to slack off and I will be just as attentive to my job as you should be to yours. Are there any questions before we begin?"

Missy leaned to Rube and mumbled, "I wonder if he needs any help with that stick."

Heinrich cleared his throat and stared directly at her. "You have a question, Miss Beechworth?"

"No, sir."

Heinrich took a step toward Missy and towered over her. "Are you sure? I heard something about needing help with a stick? What stick might that be?"

Missy could see Rube holding his hands over his face. She wished she had bit her tongue. Or at least whispered better.

"Permission to speak freely, Miss Beechworth. To which stick are you referencing?"

Missy sighed. "The one up your butt, sir," she said through her exhalation.

The gathered workers attempted poorly to cover their snickers and laughter. Rube jabbed Missy in the arm with his elbow.

Much to his credit, Heinrich's face didn't even change. He simply pointed at Missy and said, "You get to go first, Miss Beechworth."

"First where?" she asked through her laughter.

"First into the Dustwaste Wellspring."

The workers all froze.

"Oh come on!" Rube cried out.

Missy's laughter faded. "You can't be serious," she deadpanned.

"I am always serious," Heinrich replied.

"That place is quarantined, man," Rube argued. "You can't send any of us there, let alone her. No one has been there in ten years since the *Indefatigable* went down trying to investigate it."

At the mention of the famous ROSE ship that reportedly crashed near the Wellspring, Missy grew tenser. She bit her tongue.

Heinrich motioned to one of the sailors on the ship, who handed him a rolled scroll.

Missy knew it was bad judging by the ROSE seal on the back. This was an official ROSE decree document.

The large seventeen-year-old unfurled and read from the scroll. "By decree of the Royal Order of Scavengers and Engineers, Baron Hans von Deutsch is granted sole and exclusive rights to re-enter the previously quarantined area in the proximity of the infamous Dustwaste Wellspring. ROSE also decrees that Baron von Deutsch shall be unable to pursue any legal action for any losses sustained to person or property in this endeavor and wishes him godspeed on his efforts to scavenge any materials, natural or manmade, from the location. Signed, Lord Benson Fearing." Heinrich casually rolled the scroll up and handed it back to the sailor.

The silence in the air was painful. Missy looked around at her fellow workers and realized none of them were going to speak up. She already had one foot in her mouth so she might as well add the other. "And if we refuse?"

Heinrich shrugged. "Any who wish to refuse can do so and suffer the customary penalty for job abandonment."

Missy winced. The penalty for job abandonment was being docked a week's pay in addition to getting a black mark on your timecard. Three black marks and you'd never work at the Steamport Docks again. She looked around again at the other workers. They all had faces that showed them going through the same thought process she did.

"Great," Heinrich said with a clap of his hands. "We shall get on the way then. I personally think the rumors of that place are greatly exaggerated and full of old wives' tales and we have nothing to worry about. My father tells me it was well-known that Captain Hawtrey of the *Indefatigable* liked to add a little too much brandy to his morning tea, if you catch my meaning."

Of all the rumors since the *Indefatigable* went down, this one was the most widespread. Darnell Hawtrey was a brilliant airship captain, as the story goes, but had a taste for the drink and ROSE worked hard to keep him under control. If one believes the rumors, ROSE was nearly ready to strip him of his command of their flagship vessel when it went down in the dustwaste. Of course, Missy was only five when it happened, so she had no idea. The only thing she knew was her mother was a member of the crew of the *Indefatigable* and she had disappeared along with both captain and ship. Her father would never talk about Captain Hawtrey other than to say that he was a fine captain and a gentleman.

Heinrich barked orders to the crew, who threw lines and raised the sails of the large airship. The gangplank was drawn and the steam engine that powered the lift engines kicked on. The workers grumbled to themselves and said prayers to whatever deities they believed in.

Missy, however, approached Heinrich. There was no sense of sarcasm in her voice when she asked, "Are we really doing this, Heinrich?" She thought she saw a moment of doubt in his usual steadfast demeanor.

"Father says our new Faraday-shielded navigation equipment will protect us from the magnetic interference that creates such havoc around the Wellspring," he replied. There was only a hint of doubt in his voice.

"If he's so confident, why isn't he here himself?"

Heinrich exhaled through his nose and didn't reply.

For the first time in her life, Missy felt bad for Heinrich. Maybe he was an arrogant jerk, but maybe it was because he was raised by an even bigger jerk. Arrogant apples didn't fall far from the arrogant trees, or something like that. She placed a hand on his forearm and said, "Thought so." She turned and walked away from the large teenager before he could respond, if he even planned to.

Rube grabbed Missy's arm as she went below deck to join up with the workers. "What did you say to him?"

"I just asked him why his father wasn't here if he was so sure this was safe."

"Dang," Rube mumbled in reply.

"Yeah." Missy looked around at the workers. They were all inspecting their packs to keep themselves busy. In front of each of her colleagues was an array of scavenging equipment: crowbars, rope, hammers, multitools, and various other sundry bits and parts. Missy figured they had the right idea to busy their hands and try to clear their minds of the dangers facing them. She sat down and dumped her satchel onto the floor in front of her.

"What's that?" Rube asked, pointing to the ROSE flyer that was crumpled in the pile of her gear and Sprocket.

Missy grabbed it and handed to Rube. "I almost forgot," she said. "Check out the first prize. If I could win that competition, I could pay all my father's overdue bills and get him out of debt."

Rube smiled. "You really are your father's daughter."

"What's that mean?"

"People over profits," he sagely quoted. "Most kids would think of how they could spend their money on themselves. You think about how you can help someone else. If that isn't Simon Beechworth's modus operandi, nothing is."

Missy scrunched her nose up at the thought. Wasn't she just this morning scolding her father for his selflessness leading him into debt in the first place? "I'm not a kid," she answered. She waved a hand around at the assembled scavengers that included some even younger than she and Rube. "None of us are."

"What would you enter?" Rube asked, changing the subject back to the flyer.

"I was thinking about the nanomotor." She picked up Sprocket and opened a compartment on his back. She peered inside at the small motor she had been working on to power him instead of the short-lived battery cells her father used when he created him.

Rube looked into Sprocket's open back and poked a finger inside. "Is it even working yet? Have you cracked the power supply issue?"

Missy replied sadly, "Unfortunately, no. Even my old friend from Animetown is stuck on his robotic dog."

"Then the nanomotor is still theoretical?"

Missy's shoulders slumped. Rube was right. Her design for a small perpetual energy motor to power not just toys like Sprocket but mechanical tools or even small transportation machines was just that: a design. Without a working prototype, ROSE would just laugh at her as a kid with an idea that wasn't practical. And Rube was supposed to be the impractical one.

Part Four: The Dustwaste

"**S**andwall, ho! Secure your lines!" cried out a voice over the speakers in the cargo bay where the workers sat.

Everyone stuffed their gear back into their bags and satchels and lined up along the wall of the ship. They strapped themselves in with the provided harnesses and braced themselves for the impact of the dustwaste sandwall. The swirling winds of the Steamport dustwaste were so powerful, a sandstorm barrier that acted like a waterfall delineated the border between the regular desert and the dustwaste. Large airships like the *Platinschiff* could make it through safely, but to say there was a little bit of turbulence on the entry would be an understatement.

"Sandwall in five!" cried out the same voice.

Missy closed her eyes and held onto her satchel. The impact of the sand on the protective barrier the crew had raised above the ship sounded like hail on a tin roof. The *Platinschiff* rocked back and forth violently and at least two people dropped their bags. Their gear scattered all over the floor of the cargo bay. Missy clutched her satchel tighter. The tumult of passing through the sandwall faded almost as fast as it began and the *Platinschiff* steadied into a gentler but still shaky rhythm with the swirling wind patterns of the dustwaste.

"Sandwall clear!" the crewman called. "Scavengers, prepare to come abovedeck. Mind your goggles."

Missy fidgeted with her goggles before snapping them onto her face. She checked her hair to make sure there was a tight seal to prevent sand from getting inside. Nothing says fun like an eyeball full of dustwaste sand because a stray hair broke the seal. This was why Missy, like most scavengers, kept her hair short and spikey. Well, the spikey part was her personal touch. Most of them just kept it short. Rube and Missy scrambled up the ladder to the main deck and joined the crew in the swirling wind and sand.

Heinrich was standing at the controls on the upper deck.

Of course he had solid gold glasses on, Missy thought. *He's still a von Douche, after all.* She wondered how she could have felt sorry for him, even if only briefly. Besides, if something bad happened to him, it would happen to her too. Maybe Rube was right. She really was Simon Beechworth's daughter.

The ship was sailing as calmly as an airship could travel with high winds and sand swirling around its sails. Missy couldn't help but be impressed with the skill of the *Platinschiff's* crew. *I guess there's a benefit to being super, filthy rich like the von Deutsch family—you could hire the best crew.* Apparently to throw them all to their deaths, but at least they'd go to their deaths skillfully. She giggled morbidly at her own internal gallows humor.

"What's so funny?" Rube asked her.

"Oh nothing. Just thinking about how we're all going to die," she mused.

"You're a strange bird, Beechworth."

"Tweet, tweet," she replied.

The two of them sat listening to the wind and occasional calls from the crew. They had to constantly adjust the bearings, sails, and engines to keep up with the sometimes unpredictable wind stream shifts in the dustwaste skies. Missy looked down over the railing at the sand below and wondered if she could come up with a way to travel the dustwaste on land instead of air. Of course, if her nanomotor were real, the issue of no solar power to keep battery cells charged would be eliminated.

"Considering jumping?" Heinrich asked from right behind Missy and placed a hand on her back.

"What the frick, Heinrich?" she yelled and jumped away from the railing. "Why would you do that?"

"Wanted to test out not being serious for once," he mused. He actually smiled.

"You picked a real crappy time to test it," she spat. "Von Douche," she added.

"So original. I'm sure you're the first one to use that insult on anyone in my family."

"Master von Deutsch," called a nervous-sounding sailor from near the navigation equipment. "You need to see this."

Heinrich responded instantly. He ran to the upper deck and took the stairs three at a time. He reached the sailor's side within seconds. The look on his face was not reassuring.

Missy motioned for Rube to follow her and the two of them crept toward the upper deck.

"—I have no readout already, sir," the sailor was saying. "I don't think the new shielding is working."

"Did you try the magnetic field dispersers?" Heinrich asked.

"Yes. They didn't do anything. The field is too strong and unpredictable. The equipment isn't reading anything. We're about to head into range of the Wellspring region and we're flying blind."

Heinrich stared at the equipment and his eyes grew wider and wider.

Missy saw for the second time today genuine fear in the eyes of the ROSE Academy student. She'd known Heinrich for a long time, but never saw him as a regular person. Of course, when you lived the pampered noble life and never have any real struggle, it was easy to be confident and successful. The guy had no real-world stress experience to fall back on.

"Heinrich," Missy called up to the deck. "We have to turn back. You have to tell them the shielding doesn't work."

Heinrich's eyes remained frozen on the navigation equipment.

Missy couldn't believe that the uber-confident ROSE student would freeze at such a crucial moment. The ship had to turn back before the equipment was damaged beyond control. This was the very reason it was forbidden to travel into the range of the Dustwaste Wellspring. And Heinrich's hesitation was going to get them killed.

"Frick," Missy muttered and jumped onto the upper deck before Rube could stop her from doing something stupid. Once she got there, she did just that, smacking Heinrich square on the cheek.

The big teen's eyes morphed from fear to fury and he swirled on Missy. He grabbed her by the arm and lifted her off the ground, almost effortlessly.

Missy could feel her arm wanting to pop out of the socket like one of her dad's mechanical toys' limbs. The weight of her whole body strained the joint to the point of bursting, so she did the only thing she could think of in the situation and swung a foot at Heinrich's groin.

They both fell to the ground. Heinrich grabbed at his crotch while Missy rubbed her shoulder and made sure her arm still rotated. "What the frick, Heinrich? Wake up and tell them to turn us around!"

"You assaulted the commanding officer of an airship," Heinrich said flatly.

"To snap you out of your daze, man." Rube stood beside Missy now and looked prepared to defend her. Not that he could do much against the bigger, stronger, older boy.

Heinrich rose to his feet with a grunt of effort. "The penalty for assaulting a commanding officer is walking the plank," he said.

Missy let out a barking laugh. "We're sky pirates now?"

"According to the laws set out by the Royal Order of Scavengers and Engineers, assault is punishable by marooning via walking the plank." Heinrich motioned to two nearby sailors. "Grab Beechworth and Silverburg. Fit them with chutes and prepare the plank."

Rube's eyes grew almost larger than the rims of his glasses. "Why me?"

"Conspiracy," Heinrich said.

The sailor in charge of navigation raised a finger to get Heinrich's attention and said, "Sir? Maybe we should deal with that after we decide what to do here?"

"Father said we will be fine. We will not fail." Heinrich's voice was steel but, once again, his eyes gave more information. He was scared.

Missy read his eyes and realized what was going on. "You're more scared of your father than you are of whatever you'll have to face in the Wellspring. You frickin' coward!" she yelled. "I should have kicked you with both feet!"

"Sir, generally marooning happens as a punishment to force them to walk back through the desert," the navigator protested. "Sending them out here without a ship is a death sentence."

"So be it," Heinrich snarled.

The sailors looked reluctant but unwilling to disobey Heinrich's orders. They approached Missy and Rube, who were even more reluctant to try to fight off full-grown sailors that were probably as skilled in fighting as they were in sailing. Both teens were fit with chute packs and pushed toward the edge of the berth.

"Wait," Heinrich said.

The sailors looked relieved as they stepped away from Missy and Rube.

Heinrich jumped from the upper deck and stood in front of the two of them with a grin on his face. "I want to do it myself," he finished.

Then the explosion happened. The lift engine on the same side of the ship where they were standing went up in flames.

The engine on the opposite side of the ship overcompensated and forced the *Platinschiff* to list. Missy, Rube, and Heinrich all slid off the edge. Heinrich, due to his size and positioning behind Missy and Rube, flung the furthest and was sent spiraling off the side of the ship.

Missy and Rube were able to grab the railing and keep from falling off. Missy looked over her shoulder at Heinrich, who was falling fast and without a chute. She glanced at Rube, who saw the look in her eyes and protested.

"Don't do—" he began.

Missy couldn't hear him because she had already let go of the rail. The wind and sand rushed past her ears and assaulted the parts of her skin that were exposed. She tucked her arms and legs in tight and dove toward Heinrich, who was luckily slowing his descent with flailing and less aerodynamic limb positioning. She crashed into his back and spun him around in the air.

Heinrich looked up at her and his eyes grew wide behind the gold goggles. "What," was all he said.

"Hold on tight!" she screamed over the rushing wind.

Heinrich wrapped his arms and legs around Missy to the point of almost crushing her. He figured out what she was going to do and obviously knew the sudden shift of Missy opening her chute could easily dislodge him if he wasn't secured to her tightly enough.

Missy counted to three in her head then pulled the ripcord on the chute pack. As her momentum suddenly died, she felt Heinrich slip down to her legs but hold on. She was very thankful she was wearing a jumpsuit for work and not pants. That could have gotten really awkward, really fast.

Heinrich held on as though his life depended on it, because it did. The chute ride to the dustwaste below was hardly a calm journey and the two of them crumpled to a heap as they landed.

She didn't hear any bone crunching, so Missy assumed neither of them broke anything on the awkward landing. She disconnected the chute, which was immediately caught up in a gust of wind. She watched it disappear into the sand and wondered if she should have tried to hold onto the material. Her mind immediately went into scavenging mode and she assessed what she had to keep herself alive. Outside of her satchel, her assets were Heinrich and herself. It wasn't looking good.

"Why would you do that?" Heinrich asked, his voice a mix of anger and surprise.

Missy brushed the sand from her goggles and eyed the larger teen. "I just saved your life and that's your first response?" she huffed. "Don't they teach you manners at that fancy school of yours?" She slapped the embroidered rose on his uniform.

"Thank you," he stammered. "But you're an idiot. Now we're both gonna die."

Missy looked up in the air and tried to make out the *Platinschiff*. Either it went down somewhere else or they made the smart move and turned back to lick their wounds after losing the captain. Protocol stated that you couldn't afford to lose an entire ship and crew for one person and the next in command should have ordered them to turn back. She hoped Rube was okay.

That's when she saw a speck of shadow through the sand and muttered, "That fricking idiot."

Sure enough, another body was falling through the swirling winds on an open chute. She didn't have to wait long to see that Rube either lost his grip and fell or, more likely, let go to follow his friend. Loyalty, he had. Sense, not so much. Her friend's lanky body crash-landed into the loose sands a few meters from where Missy and Heinrich stood. She ignored von Deutsch and ran to Rube.

Rube disentangled himself from the ropes of his chute, and the tug of a wind gust immediately caught in the cloth and dragged him a couple of meters. He reached into his pack and pulled out a knife.

As he began to cut his chute free, Missy called, "Wait, Rube! Hold onto it!"

He looked up and saw Missy running toward him. He couldn't hear her but her arm-waving and frantic movement made him think twice about what he was doing. He smacked himself in the forehead with his free hand. Instead of cutting loose the chute, he reeled it in against the wind and quickly bundled it up so it wouldn't catch anymore.

"Smart boy," Missy said as she got closer and he could hear her. "I made the mistake of letting mine go into the wind. We may need that." She hugged Rube, then stepped back and smacked him in the chest. "You idiot."

"I'm smart and an idiot?" Rube asked. "That's next level ability right there, Missy."

"You're smart for saving the chute. You're an idiot for following me."

"Idiot see, idiot do," he chided. "When one idiot see another idiot do, the idiot do the idiot thing too."

"That makes no sense."

Heinrich called, "What are you two yammering about?"

Missy shrugged. "Idiot stuff. You wouldn't understand."

The three of them paused in silence for a moment and heard nothing but the rapidly moving winds around them. Heinrich looked into the sky. He sighed. "I wonder if the ship is lost."

Rube shook his head. "They were able to get it righted and turned around before I jumped to follow. Last I saw, they were heading back to Steamport. They were limping but moving. As far as I could see, we were the only three lost."

"We're going to die here," Heinrich said.

"If it's any consolation, you already sentenced Rube and I to die here. Kind of you to join us!" Missy said with a smile that hardly matched their dire situation.

Heinrich didn't respond. Instead, he simply glared at Missy in contempt. But also, she thought, with a hint of admiration?

"Guys," Rube called out.

Missy looked at Rube, whose eyes were wide. She could tell even through the goggles because his eyebrows were raised almost to his hairline. She turned to follow his gaze and saw what caught his attention. Through the blinding wind and sand, she could make out a structure rising from the sand. It was basically a silhouette, but there was only one thing it could be based on their location.

"It's the old spire that marks the Dustwaste Wellspring!" Missy called.

"Are you kidding me?" Heinrich responded.

Missy broke into a sprint toward the structure, not waiting to see if the boys followed. Hey, if they were going to die, they might as well see what was so special about this place before they went. And maybe, just maybe, they wouldn't have to die after all.

Part Five: The Wellspring

Missy glanced over her shoulder and saw Rube and Heinrich falling in behind her. The sprint through the loose sands of the dustwaste wasn't easy, but the exhilaration of finding the Wellspring and possibly not dying gave her the energy to push through. Rube seemed to be doing just as well, but Heinrich's large size and negative attitude turned his gait into more of a quickened trudge than a sprint.

As they neared the large metal spire that marked the Wellspring, she was amazed at how tall it was. It was also super old. The entire structure was coated in a shiny silver metal and showed minimal signs of erosion. What was this thing made of to withstand the persistent beating of a sandstorm for who knows how long?

Missy reached the spire first and walked around it, looking for an entrance. On the side opposite the one they approached, she found a door. She tried the handle and it was either locked or jammed. "Of course," she said to herself. "Find a door and can't open it. They'll find our skeletons sitting outside, wishing we had a key."

Rube made his way around the structure and saw Missy at the door. "Locked?"

** 187 **

"Or stuck. I don't know yet."

"Of course it is," Rube muttered.

"That's what I said!"

Heinrich finally rounded the corner and saw the dilemma. "Let me see your multitool," Heinrich said to Missy, who pulled it from her satchel and handed it to the large teen. He worked on the door handle with a variety of options within the multitool. The lock itself was jammed with so much sand that it was essentially pressurized into stone inside the mechanism. There was no way the lock was opening in a conventional way.

"If only I had a complex system of levers and pulleys to use," Rube mused.

Heinrich stopped messing with the handle long enough to give Rube a death stare.

He held up his hands defensively.

"Let me see your bag, Rube," Missy said suddenly.

Rube handed his backpack to her and shrugged. "Basic scavenging tools in there," he explained. "Not sure you'll find anything to use to get sandstone out of a lock."

Missy silently rifled through Rube's pack until she removed a heavy-looking wrench. "This'll work. Step back, von Deutsch."

"I don't see how a wrench is going to help," he said, backing away from the door nonetheless. "The hinges are on the inside and—"

THWACKCHING!

Heinrich stopped talking as the handle fell to the sand outside the door after Missy struck it with the wrench. She handed the wrench back to Rube and said, "Basic rule of applied mechanical engineering—any tool can be the right tool if you swing it hard enough." She pushed the door open far enough to fit through and left Heinrich and Rube outside in the sandstorm.

"I wonder if they teach that at ROSE Academy," Rube mumbled.

"I doubt it," Missy called from inside the spire.

"I guess that works," Heinrich said, following Missy through the open door.

Rube brought up the rear and walked into Heinrich's back. He had stopped just inside the door due to the absolute darkness inside. "Oof," Rube gasped.

"Give me one your flares," Heinrich called back to Rube.

Rube handed a flare to Heinrich. He sparked the flare, and yellow and red dancing lights illuminated the interior of the spire. The large structure appeared to simply be an empty metal spike as the three of them inspected what they could see. They heard nothing but the sound of wind and sand battering the shiny

** 189 **

exterior of the spire. The ground inside was made of the same metal and had a circular hatch in the exact center.

"Guess we have to go down," Rube said.

"You think?" Missy mocked. She and Heinrich grabbed opposite sides of the circular hatch door and rotated it. The mechanism moved smoothly and the door popped open with no trouble. Missy whistled. "That's some impressive workmanship to still open this smoothly after all these years."

Rube rapped his hand on the side of the spire. "Or whatever this metal is. Did you see it from the outside? No erosion, no damage. It looks like aluminum but what type of alloy is this flawless even after years of being battered by sandstorms?"

"Maybe we'll find out before we die," Heinrich grunted as he climbed down the ladder under the hatch.

"One can only hope," Missy muttered, following behind.

As the three stranded teens made their way down the metal ladder that gave off a clang with each step, the sound of the wind above slowly faded and was replaced with running water. Missy could feel her heart race. The Wellspring was actually here? The ancient water source in the dustwaste that led explorers and scavengers to their doom wasn't a myth.

Heinrich reached the bottom and jumped to the floor. It was a smoothed stone that looked natural but polished. As he swung the flare around to highlight different areas at the bottom of the ladder, the entire room looked like a smoothed-out cave. Definitely natural but also definitely further shaped by human hands.

Missy and Rube dropped to the floor behind Heinrich and joined him in searching the cavern. The ladder was at a dead-end. They could only travel in one direction, which was also where the source of the running water was coming from. Heinrich began walking.

"Wait," Missy said.

"For?" Heinrich asked.

Missy reached into her satchel and pulled out a ball of twine. She tied one end to the base of the ladder and unspooled it. "Basic rule of applied exploration—know how to get back to where you started, just in case."

Heinrich grunted but wore the hint of a smile. "You were really proud of that line to try it again?"

"I was," she admitted.

"It wasn't as good the second time."

"Noted."

Rube chimed in, "Shouldn't we mark which direction we're traveling?"

"Good luck with that," Missy said. "Check your multitool's compass."

Rube pulled out his multitool and looked at the compass. The needle spun around wildly. It would occasionally stop in a direction, only to rotate and spin the opposition way. "Oh yeah," Rube mumbled.

"I'm guessing whatever is going on down here and whatever that metal is has some serious magnetic properties," Missy explained. "No wonder our nav equipment gets all fricked around here."

Heinrich began leading the way but Rube called, "Hang on a second."

"What now, Silverburg?" Heinrich sighed.

"Why are you the leader?"

Heinrich snorted. He looked at Rube then at Missy. "Is that a real question?"

"Well," Rube started, "you'd kind of be dead if it weren't for Missy. And you did just try to kill us by marooning us in the dustwaste. Maybe she should be in charge."

"I wasn't going to maroon you," Heinrich said.

"Really?" Missy asked. "It sure felt like strapping a chute pack on us and throwing us off your airship was the first step."

Heinrich swallowed. "I had to make a point."

Rube held his hands up and waved at the polished cavern around them. "Point made?" he asked.

"It's okay, Rube," Missy said. "Heinrich. You're older, bigger, and more educated than us both. It makes sense for you to lead. I accept your apology so let's move on before we die of boredom just sitting here."

"I didn't apologize," Heinrich said.

"I accept it anyway. Lead the way, captain!" Missy said with a smile.

Heinrich narrowed his eyes then nodded. He turned and walked down the path.

Rube pushed Missy's arm. "Why would you agree to that?" he whispered.

Missy lowered her goggles around her neck and winked at Rube. "Because if there are any traps up ahead, he'll find them first."

Rube smiled. "You devious scamp."

"You say the sweetest things, my dear friend," Missy replied. She held the ball of twine in her hand and let it unravel as she walked quickly to catch up to Heinrich.

Rube picked up the rear, glancing back every few steps to ensure the twine was still secure and marking their path to the ladder.

Heinrich led them down the path and it widened as they walked.

Missy ran her fingers along the smooth walls, admiring the polished rock. It was a mix of sandstone, which didn't surprise her in a cavern under the dustwaste, and other various rocks and even metal ore. She could make out several different colors, one of which even looked like the shiny, silver-white metal of the spire above them. Whoever finished this cave did an amazing job of preserving the natural look and feel of the materials comprising the cave. It was like they put layers of metal through a rock polisher then stuck them back up to form the walls.

The sound of water grew closer and closer as they walked. They came to a fork in the path and, for the first time, Missy felt fully justified in her twine breadcrumb trail.

Heinrich stopped. He held his dwindling flare in both directions of the fork, then turned back to the others. "The water sounds stronger from the left path. I think we should follow it. At the very least, being near a water source will improve our chances of survival."

"Common sense rule of exploration," Rube began sagely, "is to go the wrong way first."

Heinrich snorted. "Maybe in those silly games you children play. In real life, we focus first on survival."

"Children? You're barely two years older than us," Missy rebuked.

"In age, not experience."

"What the frick does that mean?" Missy asked. Before Heinrich could explain, Missy held up a hand.

"Look, who cares? I agree with you that we should follow the water. Let's stop wasting time and see where this rabbit hole goes." Missy wasn't sure if Heinrich was happy or surprised that she agreed with him, but he stopped arguing either way.

Heinrich looked at his flare, their only source of light at this point, sparse as it was. "Another flare, Silverburg?"

Rube complied, handing the large, academy teen a second flare from his pack. "Only two left."

"I have four," Missy said. "We're good."

Heinrich sparked the new flare and held it up to the path on the left that clearly carried the sound of the rushing water. He looked at his dying flare and tossed it into the opposite path.

THWICK!

A pit trap on the floor a few feet from the right entrance revealed metal spikes that jutted up from the floor and impaled the flare, which finally sputtered out and left the path in darkness again. The three of them stared blankly into the darkness and shared a moment of silence.

"Good thing I know to check for traps," Heinrich whispered to Missy. Then he winked. It was weird for him to suddenly show a sense of sarcasm, considering the situation.

Missy gulped and smiled weakly. "All praise our fearless leader," she offered.

Heinrich shrugged and stepped into the left-hand path and continued to lead. A faint illumination came from the end of the tunnel in front of them. Missy and Rube once again followed behind. The sound of rushing water was even louder once they were inside the tunnel. It closed in around them like the original tunnel and forced them to stick close together in line behind Heinrich.

"It sounds less like a stream and more like. . ." Missy trailed off.

"A waterfall," Rube finished.

Heinrich stopped abruptly and the three of them bumped into each other softly.

"What the. . ." Heinrich began.

Missy and Rube peered around the larger boy and were completely stunned. Missy nudged herself in front of the other two to get a better look. The tunnel ended and there was a rush of water not ten feet below them, flowing from the polished rock like a faucet. The sink, in this metaphor, was actually a giant underground lake. The silver-white metal speckling the polished walls reflected like nightlights and gave a dim illumination of the large lake. The hundreds of small lights gave the lake an appearance of a clear night sky—the kind captured by old poems and paintings before the stars were blotted out by smog and pollution.

All this was enough to take in. This wasn't what caused Heinrich to stop and become speechless, Missy guessed. No, that honor went to the large and gorgeous and completely intact airship sitting anchored in the middle of the lake. The former flagship of the ROSE sky armada, *The Indefatigable*, was nonchalantly moored to a dock jutting from the opposite side of the lake. And it was decidedly not destroyed.

Part Six: The Indefatigable

If Missy thought the von Deutsch's *Platinschiff* was an impressive airship, it was only because she never before saw *The Indefatigable* in person. It was nearly twice as large as the ship in which they'd traversed the dustwaste. It had three masts to the *Platinschiff*'s dual-mast design and an entire additional deck. The gun ports—closed at the moment—were massive, suggesting they hid some large artillery behind them.

"Pictures do not do that ship justice," Rube said, breaking the awed silence.

"You can say that again," Missy replied.

"Pictures—"

"Shut it, Silverburg," Heinrich interrupted.

The three of them returned to silence as they continued to gape at the ship.

Missy had a sudden thought and her eyebrows rose. "If the ship survived, do you think the crew might have?"

"For ten years?" Rube asked. "I know where you're going here, Missy, but I wouldn't get too excited."

"We need to check it out," Missy said, ignoring Rube's concerned warning. She looked down at the underground lake and guessed it was about thirty meters down from the entrance. She didn't see any handholds or other ways to climb down to the lake.

"Beechworth, what are you thinking?" Heinrich asked warily.

"I'm thinking I want to inspect that ship," she replied. Then she jumped off the edge of the tunnel and plunged into the water below a few seconds later. She broke the water tension with her feet and felt surprising warmth from the lake. It was like a hot spring. She swam to surface and looked up. "You coming, boys?"

Heinrich and Rube stood at the edge of the opening above her and looked down. "You're insane," Heinrich called.

"Also," Rube added, "you missed something important." He retrieved and unfolded the chute he smartly saved from their descent from the *Platinschiff* earlier in the day. He pointed above his head. "There's a zipline here."

Missy could faintly make out a cable attached to the wall of the cave above the opening. She sighed. Of course Rube would notice something involving cables and pulleys.

Rube used his multitool to cut the chute into two strips. He handed one to Heinrich then slung his portion over the zipline cable as a makeshift pulley. Rube jumped from the edge and held firmly to the cloth, riding the cable across to the dock and landing surprisingly gracefully next to *The Indefatigable*.

Heinrich mirrored Rube's use of the chute cloth and was quickly standing beside the scavenger on the dock. The two of them looked at Missy and smiled.

Missy still didn't like seeing Heinrich smile. It was unsettling. She was also wet for apparently no reason. She swam toward the dock and the two boys helped her out of the water.

"Aw thanks, boys," she said. "Let me show my appreciation!" She gave Rube a soggy hug and enjoyed feeling him squirm as she transferred as much wetness as she could to him. She turned to Heinrich.

"Appreciation accepted," he said, holding out his hand.

Missy wiped her hand on her soaked jumpsuit and gave Heinrich a wet slap, only to pull him in for a hug as well. "You're not nearly as bad as you let on, you big lout." She looked past Heinrich and smiled. "Let's go explore the ship!"

A gangplank led down from the ship but looked unused. As Missy walked up the ramp, her hope that there might somehow magically still be people on board diminished immediately. From the distance before she jumped, the ship looked immaculate. As she stepped onto the deck, the layers of dust gave away that this ship had been untouched for a long, long time. As her shoulders slumped, she felt a hand rest on one.

"I'm sorry," Heinrich said. "I understand your mother was part of the crew, right?"

Missy turned, surprised that the empathy came from Heinrich and not Rube. "I knew it wasn't a realistic hope that the crew would be alive, but neither was finding this ship fully intact and sitting docked in a giant underground lake in the dustwaste."

"I get it," the older boy said. "Of course, there are also no corpses or skeletons. They definitely aren't here, but that doesn't mean they're dead like we all thought."

"Not sure it's better or worse to have that hope," Missy said.

The moment was cut short by Rube tripping and falling onto the deck and knocking over a table. The gangly teen scrambled to gather himself and right the table. He brushed dust off himself and then, for good measure, the top of the table. He grinned sheepishly and knocked on the tabletop. "Good craftsmanship. I've broken far worse tables than this."

"Of course it's good craftsmanship," Missy answered. "This is *The Indefatigable*. That's not just a clever name." She waved a hand in the air, gesturing to the airship around her. "This is the best ship ROSE ever crafted. It's flawless!"

A sudden crack of breaking wood hit the air, followed by a splash.

Missy turned to see a portion of the railing broken and Rube no longer standing on the deck. She ran to the broken portion of the railing and looked down at her friend, who was treading water.

"Flawless, she says," he muttered.

"Practically flawless?" she offered.

A floatation device flew over Missy's head and landed in the water next to Rube. He grabbed onto it as Heinrich pulled the now soaking wet Rube up the side of the ship and onto the deck.

"Thanks," Rube said.

"If you try to hug me, I'm throwing you back in," the burly ROSE Academy kid answered. He turned to Missy. "Flawless or not, we have to see if she's able to fly. As unlikely as it may seem, finding this ship might save our lives. Assuming it even works anymore."

Rube squished in place as he got to his feet. He looked up and around. "Even if it can fly, how do we get out?"

Missy followed Rube's eyes and scanned the ceiling of the cave as well. As far as she could tell, there were no other entrances to the cavernous underground lake. Maybe there were other tunnels like the one they followed from the spire entrance, but there was definitely no sign that any ship, let alone one as big as *The Indefatigable*, could fit through.

"Think like an engineer, Silverburg," Heinrich commanded.

Rube shrugged. "Hit it with a wrench?"

Heinrich sighed.

Missy answered, "Solve the problem in front of you first. If we can't get the ship airborne, it doesn't matter if it can't get out. No sense solving a backend problem first."

Heinrich pointed to Missy and actually gave her a thumbs-up. "Well done, Beechworth. If we had the resources, we could divide and solve them simultaneously but we only have the three of us."

"Isn't the whole divide-and-solve strategy also a good way for the team on the back end to blame the team on the front end for issues with end results?" Missy asked.

"And vice versa?" Rube added.

"Sometimes," Heinrich admitted. "Maybe you're right, Silverburg. How about you work on finding a way for the ship to get out and Beechworth and I will check out the lift engines?"

Missy clapped her hands. "Then we can blame Rube when we all die!" Her final handclap echoed in the immediately silent cave.

The two boys stared at Missy.

"Gallows humor getting a little old, huh?" Missy asked.

"A little bit," Heinrich said.

"Yes," Rube added.

"Spoil sports," Missy admonished. "Fine, we're all gonna live and make it back home. Better?"

Rube held up his hand and wiggled it back and forth in a *kinda* motion.

"In all seriousness," Heinrich said, reverting back to his commanding-officer tone. "We do need to see about actually surviving this mess."

"Is now an appropriate time to reiterate the fact that you flew us into the storm while simultaneously trying to throw the two of us overboard?" Rube asked.

"No," Heinrich answered, "it is not an appropriate time for that."

Rube saluted. "Okay, just checking. You two go check the engines. I'll inspect the dock and see if I can find anything down there."

"Thanks, Rube," Missy said. She watched as Rube sloshed his way wetly down the gangplank and onto the dock. She turned to Heinrich. "I'm gonna go check the captain's quarters first and see about getting dried off."

"This is just an excuse for you to snoop around Hawtrey's quarters, isn't it?"

Missy winked at Heinrich and pointed a finger to her nose.

Heinrich shrugged. "I'm going to see about the engines and whether or not we can even fly this ship. Don't waste too much time checking out Hawtrey's liquor selection."

Missy made a rude gesture at Heinrich and walked away. She wasn't sure why she felt defensive of the presumed dead captain of *The Indefatigable*. If anything, she should hate him if the rumors were true and her mom died on his crew because of his alcohol-infused poor judgment. Maybe it was because her father refused to speak ill of him. Then again, Simon Beechworth never spoke ill of anyone.

She found the captain's quarters on the main deck and ran her fingers across the stylized lettering spelling out "Captain Hawtrey" on the solid wooden door. The day had been so crazy so far that she only just was accepting that she was standing on *The Indefatigable*, mostly intact, and at what seemed to be the center of the Dustwaste Wellspring. She took a deep breath and opened the door to Hawtrey's bunk.

The layers of dust inside the large room mirrored the outside. There's no way anyone had been in here in a long time. Was it ten years of dust? Missy had no idea if there was any way to tell. Was dust like a tree? Were there rings you could count to see how long it had accumulated? She shrugged off the thought as irrelevant and made her way to the head.

She glanced around along the way and saw that the room was fairly standard fare for a captain's quarters on a ROSE ship. There was a sitting area with a thick table bolted to the deck where the captain could work on charts or have a meal with a few of his crew or visitors. A large, four-post bed sat across the room, with a sliding door partition available to separate the sitting area from the bedroom. Nothing seemed too out of the ordinary.

In the bathroom, she found some towels that were actually not covered in dust and tried to dry her hair. She looked in the mirror and saw her black spikey hair had gone flat from her impromptu swim. She removed her goggles and unpacked her satchel to check on all the gear inside. Sprocket came to life as she powered him up and placed him on the ground. Even though he was mechanical and had fancy additions from her Animetown friend, he was completely waterproof and functioned just fine.

"Hey, buddy," she said to her clockwork cat. "Quite an adventure we've had today. Woke up this morning worried about Dad's bills and now I'm standing in Captain Hawtrey's private head on a lost ship sitting in an underwater lake."

Sprocket made a mechanical whirring sound that replicated a purr and flashed his LED eyes in a blink. She was always amazed at how much the lights gave him a sense of life that he didn't have originally.

Missy inventoried her gear and lay out rope to dry, patted down what she could with the towels, and packed away what she could. She looked at the monogram on the towels. DH they read. "Captain Darnell Hawtrey," she said out loud to no one in particular, "the type of man to have monogrammed towels? Go figure." She opened a few drawers and found nothing particularly fun or interesting in the head. It was basic and stripped down.

"Mew," Sprocket said as he exited the room.

"Yeah yeah," Missy said to the cat. "It's boring in here, I get it. I'm not sure what I expected to find."

A small crashing sound from outside the head grabbed Missy's attention. She exited to find Sprocket backing away sheepishly from a broken glass vial and some small chunks of the white metal that seemed to be everywhere in the cave. They formerly resided on the sitting room table but were now on the floor.

"Seriously, Sprocket?" she chided the mechanical cat. "You'd think father could have turned off the 'knock everything off tables' feature in you." She walked to the debris and picked up broken glass. The vial must have been empty; there was no spilled liquid or anything else to suggest it had contained any substance. She placed the broken glass back on the table, admiring the small paw prints left by Sprocket on the dusty surface.

Sprocket responded to her admonition by licking his paws nonchalantly. Mechanical or not, cats were cats.

She turned back to pick up the few pieces of metal. "Ow!" she cried out, dropping them to the ground. The metal was hot to the touch. She eyed the ore and squinted. She couldn't see anything special or different about it. Why was it hot? The spire that seemed to be made out of the same metal wasn't hot to touch. Nor were the walls of the cave that were littered with it. She tested it again and it was just as hot. "What in the world?"

Missy ran back to the bathroom, grabbed one of the wet towels, and returned to the metal that was searing the wooden floor at this point. "Come here, Sprocket," she called.

Her pet pranced toward her at his own leisurely pace. He couldn't possibly hurry or show any signs that he was responding to her call. That would be very un-catlike.

Missy opened the compartment on his back where she stored her small allowance as a child, scooped up the metal using the towels, and dropped them into Sprocket. She hoped that whatever was causing the heat wouldn't be enough to damage him, but he'd survived far worse over the years than a little warm metal.

Sprocket flicked his tail to express his annoyance but didn't seem otherwise bothered by the metal now secured in his back.

"Thanks, buddy," she said and rubbed him between his ears. She felt his back and it was slightly warm but the heat seemed to be contained. Missy walked away from the sitting area to explore Captain Hawtrey's bedroom. What she saw on the nightstand gave her more pause than when she first saw *The Indefatigable* sitting in the cave in the first place.

"Hey, Beechworth!" Heinrich's voice called from outside the door.

Missy scooped up the framed picture on Hawtrey's end table and tucked it away into her satchel. She wanted to look at it more, but something told her she didn't want Heinrich to see it. "What?" she called out to the self-appointed leader of their band.

"Come look at these lift engines. I need another set of eyes," he answered.

"The great Heinrich von Deutsch needs a simple toymaker's daughter to help him with a big, bad engine?" Missy mocked. "Hang on, let me record that with Sprocket so I can save it to show everyone when we get home."

"Weren't you the one who kept saying we were going to die here?"

"Consider myself converted to the optimistic side," she said. "I've decided we aren't going to die here. We have to get home."

"What changed?"

Her hand went to the small bulge in her jumpsuit pocket. "I'm not sure yet," she answered. "But let's go see that engine!" She grabbed Sprocket from the table as she left Hawtrey's bunk. He still felt slightly warm but not burning hot. His body seemed to still be containing the heat from the metal.

Heinrich led Missy to the engine room. It was absolutely pristine. Being in a contained section of the deck, the accumulation of dust that collected in the upper decks was virtually non-existent.

Missy whistled. "That's some pretty mechanics right there," she added.

"That's what I said," Heinrich agreed. "Two ROSE Gen III Rankine engines power this ship. They are top of the line even compared to current models. And they're ten years old."

"Awesome! So let's fire them up!"

"We can't."

Missy glared at Heinrich. "Why not? They look flawless. I don't see a single screw out of place. I bet they still work fine."

"I bet that too. But we have a big problem." Heinrich walked to a large storage closet in the engine room and opened it. It was nearly as pristine as the rest of the room. This wouldn't have been a problem if it weren't for the fact that it was the coal storage room. He bent down, picked up a small black rock, and tossed it to Missy.

She caught the rock and saw that it was a small piece of coal. Her heart sank. "Rankines are coal engines. Everything else can be fine and dandy but with no coal?"

"No fuel, no fire, no steam, no lift," Heinrich rattled off. "Whatever happened to the crew here notwithstanding, they may have ended up here with no more fuel and then they were just plain stuck. So unless you can find a way to make that," he pointed to the small lump of coal in Missy's hands, "give off enough heat to get this engine fired up, we're stuck too."

"Why don't we just burn something else?" she proposed.

"Like what? Our clothes?"

"Like anything!" Missy said excitedly. "There's plenty of wood. Furniture. Counters. Railings. Whatever. We want to survive, right? Who cares if we have to burn half the ship to get it going? Think more like a scavenger, Noble Boy!"

Heinrich scratched his strong chin. "I suppose. Nowhere near as efficient a fuel as coal, but we can get the heat to get the engines going. It's not ideal, but it may work."

"Not ideal? Frick, man, have you ever had to do something with just the materials you had in front of you? What type of engineering training is that school giving you?"

Heinrich looked down at his ROSE Academy patch.

Missy answered for him. "The rich kid kind where nothing ever goes wrong, that's what type." She looked around at the engine room and saw plenty of tools available. The combustion chamber was secured in the center of the room and fed steam to both engines. It was clearly designed for coal and its exhaust system didn't account for burning wood. There was no grate over it to protect against ash and the unpredictable pops of a wood fire versus a coal fire. "All right, here's the deal, cake eater," she chided. "You get this firebox ready to accept wood. Find something to use as an ash guard and make sure we don't accidentally set the whole ship on fire."

Heinrich looked down at Missy. "And you'll be doing what while I do this?"

"Doing what scavengers do best! I'm gonna go break a bunch of stuff to use in a manner in which it was never designed to be used." She reached up and booped Heinrich on the nose. She then picked up a fairly large hammer from the tools scattered near the engines and went off in search of things to break.

"Crazy girl," Heinrich said with a smile.

Part Seven: The Way Out

By the time Missy returned with armfuls of broken chairs, tables, railings, and other assorted incendiaries, Heinrich had already worked to modify *The Indefatigable*'s firebox to be safer while acting as a wood-burning device. He was securing the hinges of a makeshift ash guard to the opening when Missy dropped the first batch of wood at his feet.

"Nicely done, von Deutsch!" she said without sarcasm. "We may be able to make something useful out of you yet." As she looked further, she was legitimately impressed. He had done more than craft the guard. He rerouted some of the piping in the room to serve as a more efficient flue. Coal smoke was generally way more contained than wood smoke.

"Considering we are working with painted and lacquered materials," Heinrich explained as her eyes followed the rerouted ductwork, "I wanted to make sure we didn't get a fire going only to die from inhaling the fumes in a contained room."

"I see that," she said. She patted Heinrich on the back and smiled. "Seriously, man, good work. I think we might just get out of this yet."

Heinrich grinned briefly then let it fall. "Let's not get too far ahead of ourselves. These engines look pristine but as far as we know, they haven't been maintained in ten years. Not to mention we still have to find a way to get this giant ship out of the cave, hope we have enough fuel to get lift and make it home, and see if it is even possible for just three of us to crew this monster."

Missy sighed. "You are a fun-sucker."

"A what?" Heinrich asked.

"A fun-sucker. A creature that exists just to suck the fun out of things. Can't you take a compliment, enjoy whatever small victory you can get, and move on from there? You done good, kid." She patted the combustion chamber for good measure. "You're allowed to be proud, man."

Heinrich simply shrugged.

"Come on, put those big muscles to use and help me carry more wood down. We're gonna have to load up this room with a ton before we can even get started."

Heinrich followed Missy out of the engine room and the two of them made their way back to the main deck. He was impressed with Missy's level of destruction when he saw how much wood she was able to pile up on the deck from important but nonessential materials. Much of the railing was already gone and he could see bits of chairs and other furniture in the pile.

"You are really good at breaking things," Heinrich said.

"What do you think we grunts do on the ground at a scavenging mission while you fancy lot sit on cushions and watch from the air?" she joked. There was enough truth in the joke to throw a sting into it, but she was jesting nonetheless.

Heinrich's response let her know he understood. "How else can we keep our noble bottoms from getting all sore and uncomfortable?"

Missy glared at him.

"The powder only goes so far," he added with a big smile.

Missy blinked. "Wait. Was that a joke or do you really powder your bottom?"

"Are you hitting on me, Beechworth?" Heinrich asked with a wink. He bent down to the pile of wood and lifted a massive amount in his large arms, then turned and walked back toward the engine room with it.

Missy, for the first time, was left speechless. She reached down to her left wrist with her right hand and felt her pulse quicken. "What the frick?" she said to no one in particular. "What is going on here?" She was so glad Rube wasn't around to see her getting frazzled over a boy. A handsome, strong, and smart boy, sure. But still. Eew. Speaking of. Where was Rube?

"You gonna make me carry all this myself?" Heinrich asked.

Missy started. She didn't realize he'd already returned from carrying one load and was picking up another. "Yeah. Not very gentlemanly of you to make a lady do all that physical labor."

"If you're a lady, I'm a dustwaste worm," Heinrich scoffed.

"Maybe I am," she chided.

A silence hung in the air as Heinrich looked from Missy to the docks. "Should we start worrying about Silverburg yet?"

"I was just thinking that," she agreed.

"I sure hope he isn't just taking a nap or something. If we can't figure out a way out of this cave, no amount of scavenging or engineering will help us."

"I kno—" Missy began to confirm. A mechanical whirring sound filling the cavern stopped her mid-word. She and Heinrich moved closer together and prepared to face who knew what. The entire underwater cave reverberated with a grinding metal-on-metal sound that was absolutely massive. The water sloshed in the lake and the boat rocked heavily.

"Grab on!" Heinrich called. Missy clutched onto Heinrich's midsection while he grabbed the nearest mast. "Not that I mind, but I meant to the mast," Heinrich joked.

"Shut up and be my shield," Missy shouted over the din. "You owe me!" She looked down at the ground to hide her flushing cheeks.

When the first bit of sand and debris fell from the ceiling, she had to look back up. Was the cave collapsing? All this work and survival only to have a cave-in kill them? *Not fricking cool*, Missy thought. She held onto Heinrich with one arm while snapping her goggles into place with her other hand.

Heinrich secured his goggles and also looked up at the ceiling. "I don't think it's a cave-in," he said. "Look!" he pointed to light coming from a crack in the cavern above. A dim light matching the blotted out light from the surface of the dustwaste poured through the crack in the ceiling.

As sand tumbled into the opening, Missy could make out what looked like metal teeth that were separating, creating the illusion of a crack in the ceiling. "Are you kidding me?" she mumbled.

Heinrich followed her eyes and saw the metal as well. "This isn't a cave. It's a hangar!" he cried in excitement and wonder.

"Oh, hey guys!" came a voice from the dock. "I hope I'm not interrupting anything," Rube added as he saw the two teenagers clutching one another in their shock.

Missy pushed herself away from Heinrich. "Shut up," she spat. "Is this your doing?" she asked over the metallic scraping of the hangar bay opening above them. Sand continued to pour down from the entrance into the lake and onto the upper decks of *The Indefatigable*.

"Wouldn't you know it?" Rube began. "I found this complicated system of levers and pulleys in a small building over there." He pointed back to the other end of the dock. "Thanks to my knowledge and skills, I found the mechanism to open the hangar bay."

Missy scoffed. "So you pulled levers and pushed buttons until something happened?"

"You know me so well." Rube looked past Missy and Heinrich and spied the pile of broken furniture. "And I see you broke a lot of things to reuse them for something else."

"When you have a skillset, use it!" Missy cried jovially.

Heinrich sounded optimistic for the first time as he said, "So we have fuel, a working airship engine, and a way out. Think we should see if three of us are capable of manning this gigantic ship?"

The three of them eyed the large airship and realized this was possibly one obstacle that'd be difficult to overcome.

"Is there an autopilot?" Rube asked hopefully.

"Sure," Heinrich replied. "But it can't account for manning sails and adjusting wind catch during a sandstorm." He scratched his chin. "We may be able to run just the mainsail. . ."

"You'll figure it out," Missy declared as Heinrich trailed off. She patted the larger boy on the shoulder. "We have faith in you, Captain." She turned to Rube. "Help me get this wood to the engine room so we can start setting it on fire."

"You said that way too excitedly," Rube replied leerily.

"And?"

Rube sighed and hefted some of the scavenged fuel.

Missy joined him and the two friends hauled wood to the furnace. Heinrich followed behind, carrying twice as much material as either of the others. Missy scoffed as she looked over her shoulder. "Show off."

"It's not showing off. It's helping," Heinrich said. The grin on his face belied this statement.

Once all the scavenged wood was collected in the engine room, Missy ran through her mental checklist. Fuel. Ship. Exit. Survival wasn't nearly as long of a shot as she originally thought when they fell off the *Platinschiff* just a few short hours ago. She had been trying to play it cool around Rube and Heinrich, but she really was afraid they were going to die at first. Now? Maybe they could pull this off.

"I'll have to man the steering," Heinrich began. "One of you two will need to man the mainsail. If we keep the other sails down, we won't have to worry about countering the swirling winds and can only worry about catching what we need on one sail." He paused. "Do either of you know how to man a sail?"

"Levers and pulleys," Missy answered. She pointed a thumb at Rube. "This guy's your man." Missy looked at the furnace and the pile of wood. "Guess I'm on coal shoveling duty," she assented. "Well, wood shoveling, as it is."

Heinrich nodded. He walked confidently toward the door and turned before leaving. "Missy, Rube. I'm sorry." He exited the room before the other two could reply.

"What did you do to him?" Rube asked.

"Huh?" Missy replied, still stunned at Heinrich's apology.

"I leave you alone for a little bit and when I come back, you're hugging him and now he's acting like an actual human. Did you implant some sort of chip in his neck?"

"I wasn't hugging him."

"So you did implant a chip then?" Rube said with a grin.

Missy narrowed her eyes. "Go get the sail ready. I'm gonna start the fire."

"I'll let you know if I find some marshmallows," Rube said with a laugh. He left the room with a final wave and headed above deck to the main mast.

Missy sighed and opened the furnace door Heinrich had modified. He really had done some great work. She slid open the ash guard and threw a few pieces of what used to be furniture into the furnace where coal should have gone. She scoured the room for something to use to light the fire. She spied a small acetylene torch mixed in with the tools Heinrich had used to retrofit the furnace. When she picked it up, however, it felt light. She opened the nozzle and snorted. It was out of oxygen.

"Oh frick this," she swore, reaching into her satchel and removing her last flare. She pointed the flare at the furnace, removed the cap, and struck the ignition button. The small flame dove at the wood and Missy was surprised at how easily it caught. For good measure, she simply tossed the flare into the furnace, loaded more wood, and closed the ash guard. She waited and watched the temperature gauge as it climbed past eight hundred degrees. More than hot enough.

A hissing sound reached her ears and she released her breath in time with the steam in the pipes.

"How we doing down there, Beechworth?" Heinrich's voice called through the intra-ship communication system.

Missy looked up at a speaker mounted on the wall above the left engine. She followed its wiring to another box below it. Pressing the button, she answered, "Fire lit, Captain. Sounds like we have steam going. Crank her up!"

"Roger," Heinrich replied in his *commanding-a-ship* voice. "Looks like Silverburg has the mainsail under control. He really is a whiz with pulleys and levers. Let's get this bird in the air. Over."

Missy knew her task at this point. She checked the readout. It still registered over eight hundred degrees. All she had to do was keep the fire fed to ensure it stayed hot enough to keep the water boiling. The steam would do the rest of the work.

Heinrich must have started up the engine from the control panel above, because Missy could hear the pistons start going and the hiss of steam being released into the engine. As big as these lift engines were, they were surprisingly quiet. Good old ROSE engineering. She wasn't an expert on the engines, just the general theory of steam power applied across Steamport. Heat water. Create steam. Move pistons and turbines. Convert kinetic energy into power. Engine goes.

Heinrich's voice broke her train of thought. "Keep that fire fed. We're about to lift!"

Missy looked at the furnace. The readout was dropping already. This wood was burning way too fast. She opened up the firebox and threw some more in.

She frowned at Heinrich's intervention. He obviously had a gauge of his own to track on the master control panel. She walked to the com box and pushed the button. "You do your job, don't micromanage me!"

After a moment of silence, Heinrich called back, "Part of my job is managing you."

Missy pushed the button to reply but figured it wasn't worth it. Partially, he was right. Mostly, she didn't want to admit that he was right. She shoved more wood into the firebox and swore at the ash she kicked up while doing so. The temperature rose and the engines continued purring.

"Secure the lines," Heinrich bellowed as the ship lurched upwards.

Missy looked to the ceiling of the engine room and spied the lines running along tracks for the engine crew. She cursed as she realized she couldn't reach the lines and should have asked Rube or Heinrich to get one down for her before they left. She scoured through the pile of wood and found a nicely curved piece that used to be the arm of a chair. It took her a few tries, but she was able to jump and catch her target harness and pull it down to the floor.

As she secured her line, the ship rose up from the water and her footing was lost as she unsuccessfully tried to transition from sea legs to air legs. Her satchel tumbled open, spilling out the contents. Sprocket looked especially irate at being disturbed.

"Sorry, pal," she called to her cat.

Sprocket turned his back on her and showed off the most oddly anatomically correct portion of himself: the gear that represented his sphincter. Missy never quite understood why her father felt the need to add that feature—a mechanical cat did not need a butthole—but Sprocket sure knew how to use it to express his dissatisfaction from time to time.

Missy focused on getting her harness attached and regained her footing. She was glad there was no video monitoring of the engine room from the control panel where Heinrich was no doubt standing tall and proudly steering the ship. Or was there? Missy glanced around the room and couldn't find any obvious signs of cameras. Then she stopped and wondered why she even cared.

"*Mew*," Sprocket whirred at her. He tapped the furnace with a paw, making a metal *clang*.

"Oh, you have a critique about how I do my job too?" She groaned.

She shoved more of the wood into the firebox, closed the guard, and examined her supply of wood. Missy hoped that once the air above caught the ship and the lift engines could idle so she wouldn't need to go through as much fuel as she had gone through just to get the ship airborne. After walking to the porthole on the starboard side of the engine room, she peered out to watch the underground lake shrink below as the ship rose.

Sprocket nudged Missy's leg with his head. "*Mow?*" he asked.

"I'm okay, buddy," she said, patting Sprocket's head. "Just a lot on my mind." She reached into the pocket of her coveralls and removed the picture she took from Captain Hawtrey's room. Missy ran her fingers over the picture of the handsome, swashbuckling ROSE airship captain and traced her fingers over the beautiful woman who had the same eyes as her. They were both looking down at a fairly new infant girl with familiar-looking spikey black hair. She ran her fingers through her own spikey black hair. Her free hand them moved to her goggles as she spied an identical pair around her mother's neck. The same pair? She did find these goggles in a box at the toyshop and fell in love with them years ago.

"Someone's got some explaining to do when we get home, Sprocket."

Sprocket nuzzled Missy's leg again. She could feel his extra warmth through her jumpsuit. A change in light from the porthole regained her attention. *The Indefatigable* had breached the hangar opening and was rising into the dustwaste for what Missy assumed was the first time in ten years. They might just make it

home to seek the explanation she now desperately
needed.

Part Eight: The Journey Home

"I need more steam down there, Beechworth!" Heinrich called over the coms.

Missy threw the last pieces of scavenged wood into the firebox and slammed the door shut. "I'm giving her all I got, Captain!" she returned.

"What does that mean?" the ROSE student asked.

"It means I got nothing left to burn unless you want me to start throwing my clothes into the firebox!" The lack of immediate response from Heinrich caused Missy's ears to get warm. She checked the room again for cameras.

"That would be ridiculous," Heinrich answered seriously. "Your clothes will generate pretty much no heat and how would I explain a shipmate in her underclothes to the dockmaster when we return?"

"Why can't we idle the engines?" Missy asked, ignoring the question of whether or not Heinrich was joking. "Can't we ride the wind now?"

Heinrich sounded annoyed when he replied. "If we weren't in the dustwaste, sure. If we had all the sails up and a full crew, sure. As it stands," he continued, "I need to use the engines to keep us balanced while Silverburg struggles to keep the mainsail up to give us propulsion. In all honesty, I'm surprised we haven't crashed yet."

The ship had been sailing in the winds of the dustwaste for nearly an hour and as far as Missy could tell, they were making good time. Of course, she was stuck in the engine room with a few tiny portholes and everything outside looked the same, so she had no basis for that opinion. "You are so inspiring, Captain von Deutsch!"

"Well, use that inspiration to keep the steam rolling and maybe we won't walk the last fifty kilometers out of the dustwaste! Over."

Missy assumed the conversation was over at that point. She ran through the inventory of what they hadn't already burned that was nonessential to keep the ship in the air. She thought about Captain Hawtrey's quarters. She had already broken down the sitting room furniture but the giant bed was still there. "Well, guess that's that," she said to no one in particular. She disconnected her line and picked up what she now viewed as her hammer-o-breaking-stuff from the tools.

A lurch in the ship jerked Missy free from her harness and the contents of her satchel spilled out onto the floor yet again. Sprocket mewed angrily at her for the sudden shift in his comfort level.

"I'm not too happy about it either, buddy," Missy agreed. She collected her belongings and yelped when she grabbed Sprocket. "Frick, boy," she yelped. Sprocket had gone from warm to hot since she'd put him away.

"*Mew?*" the clockwork cat whined.

Missy wrapped her hands in some rags she found with the tools and picked up her cat. She could feel the heat even through the rags. "Poor baby. You're burning up." *Can mechanical animals get fevers?* She opened up the hatch on his back and a red glow poured out onto her face. The heat was tangible. She quickly dumped the red hot metal she had stored there onto the floor of the engine room.

"*Meow,*" Sprocket said in relief.

Missy didn't have time to hope Sprocket was okay because the hot metal started boring a hole into the wooden floor. "Frick," she swore as she grabbed at it with her rag-covered hands. The heat pulsed through the rags and she looked for a place to safely store it. Her eyes landed on the firebox. She quickly kicked open the ashguard and tossed in the metal.

What happened next was amazing. Missy's eyes widened as the temperature readout on the furnace climbed back up and the steam hissed through the pipes again.

"Good job, Beechworth," Heinrich bellowed through the coms.

"Sure thing, boss man," Missy replied. She stared into the firebox and watched the metal radiate heat. "What is this stuff?" she asked to no one in particular.

"*Mew*?" Sprocket answered.

"Sorry about that, boy." Missy bent over and rubbed Sprocket's chin. The mechanical cat stretched and appeared relieved. "I didn't know it would keep getting hotter. Did you do something to it?"

Sprocket didn't answer. He just rolled onto his back and waited for belly rubs.

Missy obliged. Even his underside was still warmer than usual. She was thankful that the lurch in the ship set in motion events to get the metal out of her cat. Who knew how much damage it could have done to him? She stood up and stared at the firebox again. The temperature was holding steady at over a thousand degrees. It was hotter than the wood fire by a good bit.

She looked back to Sprocket. "Rest up here, Sprock. I'm gonna need to get more wood for when this dies down. Keep an eye on the firebox, though," she added. This was one area where Sprocket outshined a regular cat. Missy could use him as a spycat due to the small optics built into his head. She reached into her satchel and removed the standard-issue handheld com device and fiddled with a few buttons on it. A small screen now displayed what

Sprocket could see. "Thanks, buddy," she said before picking up her hammer and leaving the room.

On the main deck, she found Rube standing within what she could only describe as a marionette contraption. He had rope tied to each of his four limbs and was dancing around on the deck with them. Only when she followed the ropes did she see what he was doing. The crazy scavenger was able to control different parts of the rigging on the main mast with each limb and ran the ropes through a series of pulleys to reduce the physical effort needed.

"I've heard of a one-man band," Missy joked, "but a one-man rigging crew?"

Rube shifted his left foot and the mainsail adjusted to match a new gust of wind. "A little busy here, Missy. Shouldn't you be tending the fire?"

"Sprocket's watching it for me. Don't worry."

"We are barely keeping this ship in the air and you think telling me that your cat is watching the fire is going to reassure me?" Rube scoffed while twisting his right arm in the air.

Missy held up her com and showed it to Rube. Sprocket was still watching the firebox, thankfully. "See? Plenty of heat in there."

"What the frick are you burning? It's yellow. Certainly not wood." Rube slid his right foot back and then forward again as the mainsail tugged on his puppet strings.

"I have no idea. I didn't even burn it. I'll tell you more later. There wasn't much of it so I need to get more wood." She held up her hammer. "Time to go break a perfectly good bed!" She waved the hammer at Rube and headed off toward the captain's quarters.

"Beechworth!" Heinrich's voice called from all around her.

Missy looked around. "Yes?" she asked into the air.

"We're a few klicks away from the sandwall. Get ready to kill the heat. We can save the engine and ride the wind once we're through," Heinrich explained.

Missy sighed at her hammer. "Maybe next time, my friend." She passed by Rube and felt both amused and appreciative of her friend. As funny as he looked, he was handling his job like a pro. She waved and took off back toward the engine room. When she arrived, Sprocket mewled his annoyance for having to do something useful and climbed into a nearby box to curl up.

"Sorry to inconvenience you, buddy," Missy quipped. The lack of answer suggested Sprocket had already powered down. Missy eyed the firebox and was shocked. The heat hadn't let up at all. She peered inside at the yellow-hot metal and couldn't understand what she was seeing. It appeared to be the exact same size as it was when she first found it. "What could generate so much heat without being used up?" she mused out loud.

"Sandwall ho!" Heinrich bellowed through the ship's coms. "Secure your lines!"

"Frick," Missy spat as she hurriedly connected herself to the harness. She glanced over at the box with a sleeping Sprocket and hoped he was braced for the sandwall impact. Then she thought of poor Rube out on the main deck. He was secured, sure, but there was no way he wasn't going to feel the impact of the sandwall. That was going to hurt.

The ship struck the sandwall and Missy's body tried to fly into the ceiling of the engine room. The ship was forced downward so quickly, her feet literally left the ground. The harness cinched in place and kept her from bouncing off the ceiling. Sprocket flew out of the box and was not as lucky. He clanged into the wood above and fell just as quickly back into the box with a sickening cracking sound.

"Sprocket!" she cried, frantically disconnecting herself from her harness to check on her cat. Mechanical or not, he was still her friend and he could still break. She fell to the ground as she released her bindings and scrambled to the box. She peered inside and breathed a sigh of relief. Sprocket was powered on and looked agitated at his disconnected forelimb sitting in front of him in the box. For a regular cat, this might have been deadly. Sprocket, though, could easily have a limb reconnected. She wasn't sure if it hurt him in any conventional sense, but he sure put on a show when he had to have it reattached.

"*Mew*?" Sprocket asked. He rolled onto his side and feigned passing out.

"Oh get over it," Missy replied. "It's just a ball and socket joint. Even people have them come out sometimes and are fine."

Sprocket kicked his rear legs twice then powered down.

"Drama king," Missy laughed.

"Beechworth, we're through the sandwall. Power down that heat now. We're moving too fast toward the city. Kill the engine!"

Missy's attention snapped away from Sprocket playing dead and back to the firebox. The metal was still yellow hot and showed no signs of burning itself out. How was she going to stop the heat if she couldn't touch it? When she last tried, even through rags, it was only red hot and still nearly burnt her skin. She sighed.

"Beechworth?" the academy student questioned.

"Working on it, Captain!" she called back. Missy glanced around the engine room. Maybe she could shut off the engine another way. The hot metal in the firebox was only providing the heat; it was the steam that really powered the engine. She knew what she had to do but had to figure out how to do it without cooking herself in the process. The scavenger girl picked up her trusty hammer and eyed the porthole windows. "This should be fun," she said to herself.

The window shattered with some effort. The wind rushed past and Missy could actually see the sky instead of never-ending sand. The thought that they were actually close to surviving gave her renewed strength and excitement. She couldn't wait to tell her father about this. The thought of Simon Beechworth caused her to reflexively touch her hand to the pocket with the picture she found in Captain Hawtrey's room.

"No time for that," she reprimanded herself. Wrapping her hands in rags, she braced herself for the next step in her plan to shut off the engine. She kicked at the steampipe connected to the firebox and it separated at the joint, spewing steam into the room. She grabbed the flexible pipe and quickly turned it so she could push it out the now-open porthole window. She repeated the same steps on the opposite side of the room: break a window, disconnect a pipe, and push it out the window. The engine room became much hotter but with the steam flowing out the windows, she probably wouldn't be boiled alive. That was promising.

"What the hell are you doing?" Heinrich barked.

"No time to explain," Missy called.

"Well, you're going to have to explain real soon. I made contact with the dockmaster. We are cleared to moor and they have a whole lot of questions for us."

"Great," Missy said. She stared at the metal in the firebox. "What *are* you?" she asked it.

The metal did not reply.

She had a sudden thought. She peered out one of the unbroken windows and saw they were getting pretty close to the main city but were still over sand. She reached into her satchel and took out her backup com device. It was an older model but it had location capabilities. She rummaged through the tools and picked up a pair of metal tongs. Missy opened the ashguard, plucked out the metal inside, and dropped it on the floor. She watched as it bored a hole directly through and then through the storage room beneath. Within seconds, she could see straight through the hull and into desert below. A yellow ball of hot metal shot toward the sand. She aimed and dropped the com through the hole and let it follow the ball.

"That may have been really smart or really stupid," Missy said.

"Prepare to moor!" Heinrich called. "Stay in place for a ROSE delegation to inspect before we disembark. It would seem the return of a ship thought lost for ten years has raised some suspicion," Heinrich added dryly.

Part Nine: The Homecoming

The massive crowd waiting at the docks let on that their return was hardly a secret. Heinrich and Rube expertly moored the ship at one of the airdocks to cheers from the crowd. Missy, no longer having a specific task to do, was standing on the main deck when the ROSE delegation boarded. The spectacularly dressed men and women parted ways and Lord Benson Fearing himself stood at the base of the gangplank.

Was it just this morning I saw him in the square announcing the invention contest? Missy thought to herself as the old ROSE head briskly walked up the plank and onto the main deck.

He glanced at Missy and looked immediately past her to Rube, who was still working at disentangling himself from his one-man-rigging-crew contraption. "Who is in command of this ship?" Lord Fearing demanded.

"I am, sir," Heinrich answered from the bridge. He exited the door to the steering room and presented himself with a salute and a firm arms-to-the-side stance.

"Master von Deutsch?" Lord Fearing asked. "You were reported lost by your crew just a few hours ago."

"It would seem they reported prematurely, sir," Heinrich answered.

Missy smirked. Was Heinrich actually being sarcastic? Maybe he'd spent too much time around Missy and Rube. Or maybe it was just enough time.

Lord Fearing either ignored or missed the sarcasm. "Who else is aboard this ship?"

"Just us three, sir," Heinrich answered smartly.

There was a hushed gasp from the crowd and even some of the full-fledged ROSE members who were aboard the ship. Missy's smirk got an extra layer of smugness to it.

"You sailed this ship with just three crewmembers? Two of which are simple scavengers?"

"Who you calling simple?" Missy belted out before she thought about any repercussions.

Fearing glanced at her and narrowed his eyes. The golden monocle framing his left eye amplified the intensity of his glare. "You're the toymaker's kid, right?"

Missy tried to hide her surprise that Lord Benson even know who she was. "Misanthrope Beechworth, sir," she said more properly. "I apologize for my tone, but we are not simple."

Fearing actually smiled at her. "I only meant that you were not trained crewmen, child, and if my tone was insulting it was merely out of shock and awe at what you three accomplished." He took a step toward Missy and offered his hand. "Thank you for returning the ship and I am pleased to see you all home unharmed."

Missy shook his hand and wisely, if belated, kept her mouth shut.

He pointed to Rube. "You there? What is that contraption?"

Rube stammered, "Um, I don't really have a name for it, sir."

"And your name?"

"Ruben Silverburg, sir. But people call me Rube."

Fearing walked slowly toward Rube and eyed the ropes and pulleys. He whistled impressively at the end. "Well, Rube, you might want to name it. I may have some questions for you about this. And you may want to think about entering the ROSE Inventionfest Open," he added with a wink.

"Thank you, sir."

"As for you," Lord Fearing said, turning to Heinrich. "Your father will have a lot of questions about the events of the last day. I suggest you prepare yourself for that."

Heinrich visibly winced at the mention of his father. "Yes, sir," he said, his voice unfazed.

Lord Fearing turned to the crowd at the dock and pressed a hand to his chest, where the brass rose signifying his role as the head of the Royal Order sat. It apparently was also an amplification device because his voice boomed over the crowd. "I am sure there are many questions for these three brave young souls and much gossiping about the return of *The Indefatigable*. I assure you all, we will get those answers as soon as possible. For now, return to your homes or places of business. We have this under control."

The crowd murmured and reluctantly dispersed. When most of them were gone, Lord Fearing addressed the three of them again. "Miss Beechworth and Mr. Silverburg," he began, "you should get home to your parents. I'm sure they are worried about you."

"Yes, sir," Missy and Rube said in unison.

"Master von Deutsch, you should come with me to see your father so you can debrief him on today's events."

Missy glanced over her shoulder at Heinrich as she walked down the gangplank. The large boy's shoulders were lower and his face was a little bit paler than it had been moments before. She felt bad for him and wished she had said something before she left. She settled for a wave that he glanced at but didn't return.

Lord Fearing was whispering something to him as Missy turned and made her way home.

* * *

". . .and then Lord Fearing came aboard and actually seemed really nice!" Missy finished explaining to her father.

The petite toymaker looked absolutely aghast at the adventure his daughter had just described. "Misa, how could you sound so excited about this? You nearly died."

"Oh, I was fine." Missy dismissed his concern. "But how cool was it that we found the ship and flew it out? You should have seen Rube. He looked like a puppet on strings but he operated an entire main mast by himself!"

Mr. Beechworth let a smile break through his worried veneer. "He finally found something useful to do with those ropes and pulleys, huh?"

"He sure did!" Missy screamed with laughter. "Before I forget though, dad," she added, reaching into her satchel and removing Sprocket and his disconnected limb. "Could you fix him? He took a big hit when we went through the sandwall and he's been playing dead since."

"You could easily fix him, you know. You've become quite skilled, daughter."

"I know. But I like it when you do. And I think Sprocket does too. I'm also tired and I need to sleep."

Mr. Beechworth's smile regained its usual cheer. It was that wonderful toymaker's smile that he was famous for. "Of course, Misa. Go rest."

"Thanks dad," she said, kissing him on the cheek and not even caring that he used his baby name for her. She left Sprocket with her father and went to her bedroom. Instead of lying down on her bed right away, which she desperately wanted to do, she emptied the contents of her satchel onto the bed. Amidst the usual gear she packed for a day scavenging were three new items: the hammer she confiscated from *The Indefatigable*'s engine room, the flyer advertising the ROSE Inventionfest, and the picture she found in Captain Hawtrey's room. She felt guilty leaving out the picture when she told her father the details of her adventure, but she wasn't sure how she felt about it yet. . .and whether the toymaker knew. And if he did know, shouldn't he have told her?

She put aside her thoughts about the picture and the Inventionfest to glance at her com device. Before she could rest, she had one more task to complete tonight: retrieving the mysterious metal she found in the captain's quarters that both baffled her and may have saved their lives on the flight from the Dustwaste Wellspring.

She powered up the com device and set it to begin searching for the location of her backup device that she hoped landed close enough to the metal that she'd be able to find it. The com dinged affirmatively that it had connected to the signal put off by the backup com, and her heart fluttered excitedly. "Once papa goes to sleep," she said to herself, "I'll retrieve the metal and figure out what it is."

Part Ten: The Eureka Moment

Retrieving the metal Missy found on *The Indefatigable* was easy. Her plan worked and the metal—completely white and no longer generating heat—was just a few meters away from the backup com device she'd used to mark its location. Figuring out what it was, though? That was the hard part.

Missy poured through every chemistry and organic science book she could find in the Steamport library. She searched what she could on what remained of the 'net on her com device. It was easy to track down a list of silvery white metals that matched the physical description of what she found: silver, nickel, aluminum, palladium, osmium, iridium, and rhodium. The list went on. She was able to rule out the more common metals easily. None of them reacted the way this one did.

All the research she was doing was a good distraction from the hoopla surrounding the return of *The Indefatigable*. Rube and Missy were awarded with the equivalent of a month's salary of scavenge work for their parts in the recovery. It was enough to get some of the bill collectors off her father's back for the moment, but it wouldn't last.

Heinrich, on the other hand, was given a commendation and a big shiny medal to pin to his uniform under that smug face of his. Apparently nearly killing your entire crew then trying to throw someone off your ship was a negligible detail. Of course, no one seemed to report that portion of the story. Missy figured it was for the best. Who cared what happened to a couple of Scraptown kids? The nobles had their story and that was all that mattered.

After few days of questions, ROSE seemed to forget about Missy and Rube altogether. *The Indefatigable* was being restored and prepared for a grand re-commission in the future. Star ROSE Academy student Heinrich von Deutsch would be there to break the bottle and cut the ribbon or whatever it was the noble types did for that type of celebration.

"Missy!" Rube screamed.

"What?" she asked just as loudly.

"Where did you just go?"

"Huh?"

Rube tapped his finger on the periodic table of the elements resting on the library table. All the elements on the chart they had ruled out were crossed off. "You've been just staring at this for a solid five minutes. I think you stopped breathing for a moment."

"Was just thinking."

"About Heinrich again?" Rube teased.

"Von Douche? Of course not. I just want to figure out what this is and how I can use it. It was all over the place in the Dustwaste Wellspring."

Missy had told Rube and only Rube about the metal and how it helped them stay airborne on the journey home from the dustwaste. She didn't trust anyone else with it.

"I still think you should show it to Metallurgist Winthrop. If anyone in Steamport can identify a metal, it's him."

"And if anyone can take credit for someone else's discovery, it's the nobles. And he works for them."

Rube sighed. "So you weren't thinking of Heinrich then, huh?"

Missy punched him in the arm. "Shut it," she spat.

Rube rubbed his arm reflexively. "Have you considered that maybe it isn't one of these?" Rube asked, pointing to the periodic table.

"Of course I have, you doofus. But I'd have to rule out all of them before even considering it. I really feel like it's one of these two, though," Missy said, pointing to iridium and osmium in turn.

"Why?"

"Their corrosion resistance. Remember that big spire that marked the Wellspring? I think it was made out of this metal. It was smooth even in the middle of a sandstorm. No wear, no pockmarks, nothing to show it was being battered by a storm for who knows how long."

"But osmium is blue-grey, right? Doesn't that rule it out?"

"It might be an alloy," Missy countered.

"And aren't they two of the rarest metals out there? How would enough of it to build a giant spire in the dustwaste be collected?"

Missy shrugged. "How is there a giant magnetic black hole out there? How did that ship end up underneath the dustwaste? What happened to the crew? You want to play 'ask the impossible questions' or figure out what this is?"

Rube held up his hands in surrender. "Fine. But I still say your only chance is going to the metallurgist. He's got access to better tools and equipment to calculate what's going on. Can I ask another question or will you hit me?"

Missy held up her fist. "Ask the question and then you'll find out."

"Why is this so important to you? You've never been this serious about anything. What happened to you down there? You've been different since we got back."

Missy relaxed her fist. She really wanted to tell Rube about the picture. But that was the one thing from the adventure she kept to herself. She still hadn't even asked her father about it yet.

Rube looked relieved to not be punched but concerned also. "That right there, Missy. That's exactly what I'm talking about. Where do you keep disappearing to?"

"Will you buy near death experience changing a person to take things more seriously?" Missy proposed.

"For anyone else? Yes. For you? No."

Curse you for knowing me so well. "I want to use the metal for the Inventionfest. The fact that it could generate so much heat and never get any smaller is revolutionary. It's almost magic in that it seems to break the law of conservation of matter. It's a real honest-to-goodness perpetual energy generator. Do you know how amazing that is? Mythical even."

"The nanomotor," Rube almost whispered.

Missy pointed to her nose with her index finger. "It's the missing piece. I've tested it. It works. I just need to get it heated up, and it will burn forever and never deplete, as far as I can tell. For whatever reason, sand seems to be all you need to squelch it."

"So why not just use it? Throw it in the nanomotor, show how it never loses energy or power, and call it a day?"

Missy threw up her hand. "You don't think I thought of that? ROSE is going to ask questions. They're gonna want specs. They're gonna need more than the prototype in front of them. I'm not putting on a magic show for kids. I'm trying to present something revolutionary to the smartest engineers in Steamport!"

"Good point." Rube paused and swore under his breath. "Do you think they're going to request all that for the Rigionette?"

"Glad you liked my name for it," Missy quipped.

"One-Man Rig? Maybe. But I like mine better."

"I guess," Missy assented. "But no, Rube, I don't think so. It's a brilliant application of existing technology but I think the genius of how you put it together is the unique part. The technology itself doesn't need much explanation."

Rube held his hand to his heart in shock. "You just called me a genius." He scrambled into his pack and removed his com device. "Can you say that again so I can make it my alert sound for when you com me?"

Missy shoved her friend and laughed. "Nope. Besides. I said the idea was genius, not you."

"Close enough," Rube said through a wide grin. "I'll take it." He looked at the periodic table and frowned. "I get it, though. You'll need to explain the how, not just show that it works."

"Frick it," Missy said, dumping the contents of the table into her satchel. "The Inventionfest is in a week and I need an answer. We're going with your idea."

Rube clutched his hand to his chest.

"Oh shut up."

"You must really think I'm a genius."

"I do not. I am just out of options and your idea is the best left at the bottom of the well."

"I'll take it again," Rube said with a smile. "Let's go!"

* * *

"Iridium," Metallurgist Winthrop said as he handed the metal back to Missy after running a few tests on it in his workshop. "No doubt about it. It's not a common metal but I've worked with it before. Didn't take me long to identify it."

"Pure?" Missy asked.

"As pure as I've seen in a long time. It's essentially pure."

Missy bit her lip, deciding whether or not to go next level with her trust of the old metallurgist. She knew him to be a kind man, and her father spoke highly of his skill and knowledge.

"What's wrong, Missy?" The thin older man wiped his hands off on the leather apron he wore to protect his clothing from sparks and chemicals and the other hazards of working in a metal shop. "You were telling me the truth about how you found this, right?" He eyed Missy warily.

"I did!" she answered sharply. "It was on the ship."

"Just show him, Missy," Rube said from his place in the corner of the room.

Missy jumped. She had forgotten he was there, waiting with her while the metalworker ran his tests. "Fine." She walked over to the stack of metal molds and grabbed a mini ceramic foundry from among the metallurgist's equipment. "Let me show you this." Missy placed the piece of iridium into the foundry and used a small torch to add heat to it.

"That torch won't get hot enough to do anything to iridium," Metallurgist Winthrop said. "Its melting point is well over two thousand degrees Celsius."

"I'm not trying to melt it. Watch." Missy continued to apply heat until she saw the metal start to change color. She stopped and motioned for the metalworker to look inside the foundry.

"What in the. . ." his voice trailed off.

"Still think it's iridium?" Missy asked.

"Yes, but maybe not as pure as I thought. I'd have to melt it down and separate out any impurities if it really is an alloy and figure out the makeup."

"No!" Missy shrieked louder than she expected.

"Why not?"

Missy shook her head. "Keep watching it. It will never go out. It won't stop generating heat. But the metal will never get smaller."

** 251 **

"That's impossible," the metallurgist protested.

Missy shot a glance at Rube. "Well, that answers it for us. Apparently what is happening in front of us right now is impossible." Missy reached into her satchel and withdrew a pouch of sand from the dustwaste. She poured it over the metal and it immediately stopped emanating heat.

"What did you do?" Winthrop asked.

"The only thing I have seen that can stop the reaction is sand. Any ideas why?"

The old man sat back in his chair. "It can't be. . .could it?"

"What?" Missy questioned.

"You found this in the Dustwaste Wellspring you say?"

"A ton of it. But this piece was in Captain Hawtrey's room on his table along with some others and an empty vial. My cat brought it to my attention. I think he somehow added enough heat to it when it fell to start the reaction. I nearly cooked him from the inside thinking it was safe to store it inside him."

Rube chuckled. Both other people in the room looked at him. He held up his hands. "That would sound so wrong if your cat wasn't a machine."

"Shut it, Rube," Missy said. She turned back to Metallurgist Winthrop. "Why is that important?"

"Rumors," Winthrop said. "Just rumors. But if the rumors are true, I know what we're missing. And that crazy bastard Hawtrey must have been chasing the legend. Old stories among the sky captains and nobles tell that the location of the Dustwaste Wellspring was originally a crash site of a giant meteor from outer space. Maybe twenty years ago now."

Rube moved closer to the metallurgist. "A giant space rock crashed and no one knew about it?"

"You know how good ROSE is at keeping secrets, right?" Winthrop said in a whisper, as though ROSE was in the room listening. "Only they know what really happened because only ROSE crews went out to investigate and try to scavenge. We don't know what, if anything, they recovered. After *The Indefatigable* was lost, ROSE supposedly canceled its efforts to investigate. From what I heard of your adventure, it seems they were ready to start it back up again with Baron von Deutsch taking the lead."

"Why risk it?" Missy quested.

"The metals alone from that meteor are worth it. That's why I've worked with iridium before. Most of the iridium we have comes from space, but usually in really small amounts. This meteor was supposedly loaded with it."

"So why does this one act differently than iridium you've worked with before? Is it an alloy then?" Rube asked.

The metallurgist shook his head. "Pure, as I originally thought. And I don't have an exact answer, but there's a theory that has nothing to do with metal. Well, not directly at least."

Missy rolled her hand in a *keep going* motion.

"Every meteor has a different makeup. Some have been found to have a frozen core. It's never been recorded, but microbiologists surmise that it isn't impossible that living organisms might be dormant inside the ice. I think what we have here," he said, pointing at Missy's piece of metal, "could be that."

"The alien metal has alien life forms in it?" Rube posed. "Are they really small?"

Missy sighed. "You do know what the 'micro' in microbiology means, right? Bacteria then?" she asked Winthrop.

"It's only a theory, but it's possible what we have here is a bacteria that uses the iridium as a catalyst for an internal fermentation process, but somehow doesn't consume the metal in the process. You said you found the metal in Hawtrey's room with an empty vial?"

"That Sprocket broke, yeah."

"What if the vial wasn't empty?"

Missy sat in stunned silence. Of everything that happened on their adventure to the Dustwaste Wellspring, was it possible her "discovery" of the metal was just an accident because her cat wanted to knock things off a table? She laughed out loud.

"What's so funny?" Rube asked.

"Huge scientific breakthrough caused by a cat knocking a glass off a table."

"I doubt it would be the first time," Winthrop joked.

"So now what?" Missy asked, getting serious for the moment. "If it's possible that Captain Hawtrey and the crew of his ship were there to get this and maybe already discovered this, wouldn't ROSE want that information?"

"Of course they would," Rube said.

"Are you going to report to them, sir?" Missy asked Winthrop.

"I wouldn't lie to them if they came to me, of course, but I have no intention of ratting you out, Miss Beechworth. But I wouldn't hold onto it for too long. They will no doubt figure it out, presuming there were any notes or other evidence left on *The Indefatigable* when you returned to dock."

Missy smiled. "That's all I needed to hear. I'll tell them, all right. But I'll tell them in public. The Inventionfest is coming and I can't wait to show off my invention!"

The metallurgist smiled. "Good luck. I'll be rooting for you. And be careful."

"Careful? Why?" Rube asked.

"ROSE may not like feeling like they don't have control of information. They aren't evil or nefarious or anything, but they like to keep things under control and keep everything in line. Engineers, you know. Can't abide by things they can't organize and predict."

"I will. And thank you again!" Missy retrieved her dormant metal and led Rube out of the metallurgist's shop. She practically dragged him back to her house so she could put the finishing touches on her presentation for the Inventionfest. Since Rube was basically done with his Rigionette, she enlisted his help in modifying her nanomotor specs to incorporate the iridium that possibly housed alien bacteria.

Part Eleven: The Inventing Contest

The day of the ROSE Inventionfest Open was at hand. Missy had spent a week fine-tuning her nanomotor and configuring Sprocket to be the test subject to demonstrate it for the contest. In exchange for Rube's help, Missy also gave Rube's Rigionette a once-over. She had to admit, Rube's design could have practical applications even if it did make him look like an idiot when he demonstrated it. Missy took a deep breath as she slung her satchel over her shoulder and made her way to the front door of her house.

"Misa?" her father's voice called from behind his workbench.

Missy felt bad immediately, but not because of the name he used for her. She had come to appreciate his affection lately. She still hadn't talked to her father about the picture she found in Captain Hawtrey's quarters on *The Indefatigable*. The picture, she assumed, was of her family — and her father?

"Yes?" she called back over her shoulder.

"Good luck today. I love you."

The last line gave Missy even more guilt. She resolved to talk to her father about the picture and her parentage as soon as the contest was over. He had to have known. Maybe that was why he never spoke ill of

** 257 **

Captain Hawtrey. Was he planning on telling Missy one day and didn't want to be just another person badmouthing the memory of her birth father?

"Is something wrong, Misa?" he asked, as she stood frozen.

"Not exactly. Just nervous about the contest. Hoping I don't embarrass myself." She figured this was good. It wasn't a lie — she was super nervous. People from all over Steamport, from Scraptown to The Reach, would be submitting inventions for the contest. There were no age brackets. The only people that couldn't compete were members of ROSE or academy students. Other than that, it was a full-on open forum. How could a kid expect to compete with adults, life-long scavengers and tinkerers, and non-ROSE affiliated nobles?

"I understand. But you have a brilliant mind. And your motor is brilliant. I hope your new energy source works as you expect."

"It will," she said confidently. "Thank you, father. I'll do you proud."

"You already have," he answered softly.

Missy's cheeks flushed as she waved good-bye to her father and met with Rube so they could walk to the contest together. He waited for her at the end of her spoke of the wheel just outside the central square. Rube carried a large duffel bag filled with the parts he would need to set up the Rigionette for the judges. Missy laughed as he struggled with it.

"Shut up," Rube spat. "Not all of us can make a tiny motor to put in our pet cat."

"True," Missy said, and grabbed hold of one of the handles of his bag. "Let me help you then."

The two of them walked with Rube's bag between them into the circle, where ROSE had set up a massive array of tables in rows. Prestigious members of ROSE sat behind each table. Each table was for a slightly different branch of engineering, and the members sitting at each were the unarguable experts of their field. On a raised dais behind the tables stood a podium, an amplification device, and Lord Fearing himself. A banner of metal and glasswork was raised above him, proclaiming the First Annual Inventionfest Open. The banner itself was a masterful piece of art. Lines formed at each table.

"Guess this is where we part ways?" Rube said to Missy.

"Guess so!" she answered. Her nanomotor would be judged by the table for electrical engineering, specifically the power engineering sub-specialty focused on motors and power generation. Rube would be with the mechanical engineers since his device was comprised of numerous simple machines but configured in a unique way for airship management.

Figuring out which line to get in was probably the first thing they did to weed people out.

Rube held out his hand. "Good luck, Missy. You're a genius."

Missy shook his hand sardonically and said, "You too, Rube."

Rube smiled. "You called me a genius again!" he called before picking up his duffel and scuttling to his line before she could refute his claim.

"I meant the luck part!" she screamed after him. Either he didn't hear her or simply ignored her, but the result was the same. Rube was quickly lost in the crowds jostling for position in their various lines. Missy laughed to herself. "He did that on purpose."

Missy got a chance to grow more anxious as she waited in her line. Without Rube to talk to, she was essentially alone. The events of the past few weeks ran through her head over and over again. She began with the fear that ROSE would be mad at her for withholding information about the metal she found on the ship. Was there more on the ship that she missed? Did they already have it in hand?

She fidgeted with her goggles as she took a few steps forward, realizing the line was moving more quickly than she expected. Her hand moved absently from her goggles to the pocket where she kept the picture of Captain Hawtrey with her mother and, she was pretty sure, an infant version of herself. They looked like a happy family. While Missy didn't grow up unhappy and Simon Beechworth was everything she could ever want in a father, she wondered what it would have been like growing up among the nobles instead. Why had that been denied to her?

"Come on, kid," a woman said from behind her.

Missy turned to see a middle-aged noble woman holding what appeared to be a model of a type of rotary engine. At a quick glance, she couldn't see anything particularly special or different about it but who knew? "Sorry," she mumbled before taking three large steps forward. Missy looked ahead and saw only a few people in front of her at this point. How was the line moving so fast?

She practiced in her head what Rube told her was called an "elevator speech." Rumors were that so many people were planning on attending the Inventionfest that each person would only get a few seconds to impress the initial judge at their table before being moved into the larger competition as a whole. Missy still wasn't sure how much information she should give in the initial judging. She had to be convincing enough to move on but was afraid that she'd miss her chance for a big reveal more publicly later.

A shove from behind snapped Missy out of her third space-out since Rube left. The woman with the rotary engine was apparently done being polite about her holding things up. Missy looked forward and saw she was next in line, even though she was about ten meters away.

A very bored-looking man in his fifties sat at the table. He wore traditional ROSE instructor clothing. Missy recognized him as Baron Reginald Bjorn, who was famous as both an inventor and one of the teachers at ROSE Academy. He was apparently very hard to please, if the stories from ROSE graduates and students were true.

"Name?" Baron Bjorn asked, waving lazily toward Missy to approach the table.

"Misanthrope Beechworth, sir," she answered.

His bushy left eyebrow actually rose, which was more emotion than she expected from the famously turgid professor. "The toymaker's daughter who recently helped Heinrich von Deutsch recover *The Indefatigable*?"

"From what I understand, sir, the official story is that he recovered it despite my interference," she began. "And was quite daring about it," she added with as little sarcasm as she could manage, which unfortunately was still a lot.

"So it would seem," he replied placidly. "What is your invention then?"

"A nanomotor with a power cell that, as far as I have been able to determine, produces perpetual energy."

Baron Bjorn scoffed. "So you, an untrained scavenger teenage girl, have cracked the mythological perpetual energy generation feat that has stymied engineers since humans first discovered mathematics? Your next line better be really good, Miss Beechworth, if you want to continue in this competition."

Missy reached reflexively for her goggles and stroked them. "Yes, sir. I have cracked it." She paused.

"And? What is your energy source?" Bjorn coaxed.

Missy sighed and quickly rambled, "Iridium I discovered in Captain Hawtrey's cabin on *The Indefatigable* that burns but never depletes, sir. I devised a silica-based casing after discovering that it could be activated with minimal initial spark but only quenched with sand. I housed it in this," Missy said, reaching into her bag and producing Sprocket. "My cat."

Baron Bjorn sat motionless for a moment. He leaned forward and whispered to her, "You are disqualified, Miss Beechworth. Next," he called to the woman behind Missy.

"Wait! What?" Missy screeched.

Bjorn didn't flinch. "You are attempting to submit something using a power core comprised of proprietary ROSE materials that do not belong to you. Not only are you disqualified, but also I imagine Lord Fearing will want to speak with you about this. I wouldn't stray too far, Miss Beechworth." He waved to the rotary engine woman. "Next!"

Missy picked up Sprocket from the table, who mewled at her questioningly. "Frick them," Missy said to her cat. "We'll see about this." Putting Sprocket back in her satchel, Missy made to leave from the line but instead ran full speed toward the dais where Lord Fearing sat observing the tumult of the Inventionfest with some of the higher lords and ladies of ROSE. She spied Baron von Deutsch, Heinrich's father, among them. He was laughing at something the woman next to him was saying. Missy couldn't even see who she was because a red hazed formed over her vision. She wasn't sure if she was going to cry or scream.

It wasn't fair. She got none of the credit for her role in returning *The Indefatigable*, apparently her father's ship. She was stuck with the life of a scavenger and junker instead of the life she should have had. She found a way to contain the iridium so it simply didn't burn forever, which clearly ROSE never did or they would have patented it and bragged about their ability to generate infinite power and talked about how great they were.

She reached the dais and leapt onto it. She reached into her satchel for Sprocket but didn't get any further than that as a large man tackled her to the ground and struck her with a zapper of some sort. Sprocket fell from her hand as she blacked out.

Part Twelve: The Future

Missy awoke in a bed. She looked around. It wasn't her bed. It was way too nice to be her bed at the back of the toyshop. Her head was pounding and she winced at the light coming from the halogen bulbs above her. She felt under the sheets and found she wasn't wearing her jumpsuit and her satchel wasn't with her. She had been changed into ultra-soft pajamas. That part creeped her out a bit.

"Good morning, Misa," came a voice from next to her bead. She rolled over and saw her adoptive father sitting calmly next to her. He had Sprocket on his lap and was slowly petting the metal cat.

"Are you doing a super villain thing? The smile is too nice to be super villainy."

"What?"

Missy sat up on her elbows to look at her father better. "You know, sitting there waiting for me to wake up while petting a cat. Very villain-like. Are you here to tell me that you've been expecting me and I almost foiled all your plans but wasn't fast enough?"

"What is she talking about?" came another familiar voice. She focused her eyes past the toymaker and saw Rube as well.

"Probably another story from that old camp she went to as a child. Such crazy stories she returned with," Simon Beechworth said with a smile. He focused his attention back on Missy. "No, Misa, I am here because you were stopped seemingly about to attack Lord Fearing and the other high lords of ROSE after you were disqualified from the Inventionfest. You've been out for about eighteen hours. You must have been exhausted."

"And electrocuted," she added.

"That too."

"So am I under arrest or something? I wasn't going to actually assault anyone," she said, only partly believing it herself. She really had no idea what she was going to do.

"No," a new voice came from the opposite side of her bed.

Missy rolled over and the very first thing that caught her eye was the reflection of the halogen lights off the brass rose pin worn by the head of ROSE. Lord Fearing himself sat next to Missy's bed opposite her father. He looked genuinely concerned though pompous with his golden monocle and silk top hat.

"You are not under arrest," he finished. "But judging by the items we found on your person, I think you have just as many questions as I do."

"So you strip searched me?" Missy asked, gesturing to her change of clothes.

Lord Fearing flushed.

"I changed you," her father answered quickly. "You were zapped, Misa. That much electricity running through your body tends to have certain . . . effects on various muscle control functions. It isn't so much the contractions caused by the shock as the relaxation after you pass out."

Missy facepalmed. "I peed myself didn't I?"

Rube snickered from behind her father. He stopped just as quickly at a death glare from Missy.

Lord Fearing cleared his throat and held out the picture she took from Captain Hawtrey's quarters. "I was specifically referring to this picture of your mother."

"And father?" Missy asked.

"And father," Lord Fearing confirmed. Silence hung in the air at the confirmation.

"I'm sorry, Misa," Simon Beechworth began. "I was sworn to secrecy to not tell you until you were eighteen. Until then, you were supposed to believe you were born of the lower classes like your mother and, well, myself."

"Why? What happens when I turn eighteen?"

Lord Fearing answered instead of the toymaker. "That was very dependent upon a lot of factors, Miss Beechworth. That your parents never returned was a big one. We wanted to keep you somewhere safe with someone ROSE trusted. Or, more specifically, someone I trusted. Simon and I are old friends, you see, and I wanted you to be both loved and safe."

Missy's cheeks grew warm and she looked at her father. "And I was. And am," she confirmed.

"Good," Lord Fearing said. "I also had to keep your parentage a secret, or at least the fact that Captain Hawtrey was your father, for many boring adult and political reasons. First and foremost, your father was betrothed to a noble woman when he fell in love with your mother."

"Who?"

"Not that it matters now," Lord Fearing answered, "but Greta von Deutsch."

"Baron von Deutsch's sister?"

"The very same."

A light bulb went off in her head. No wonder the von Deutsch family hated her real father so much and did everything they could to sully his name in his absence. "And why am I being told all this now?"

"Because I want to continue keeping you safe. When you turn eighteen, you will be entitled to claim your birth father's title and inheritance. I have preserved proof to defend you when you make your claim and have held back any claim from the von Deutsch family in the ROSE court system on the basis that, since your father's body was never found, he could not be presumed dead. The lack of dead bodies on *The Indefatigable* helps me continue that argument."

"Why would you do that for me?"

Lord Fearing sighed. "Because I loved Darnell like a son. Yes, he was reckless. Yes, he was impetuous. But he was a brilliant captain and an honorable man. His love for your mother was the only thing stronger than his dedication to ROSE and Steamport as a whole. When I heard that *The Indefatigable* was returning, I hoped that I would see that cocky smile once again. Instead, I found the three of you."

Missy looked past Simon Beechworth at Rube, who waved. "Why is he here?"

"Rude," Rube spat back.

"Because I have a proposal for you and him both." Lord Fearing stood. "Mr. Silverburg has already agreed to it, but said he will only agree if you do as well. He's a fiercely loyal friend, Miss Beechworth."

"And also the winner of the Inventionfest Open!" Rube called, holding up plaque with a golden rose carved on it. "The Rigionette took first place," he beamed.

Missy sighed and fell back onto her bed to stare at the ceiling. "I get disqualified and Rube won?"

"Hey, you said I was a genius."

"He really is," Lord Fearing said. "Sometimes we overthink things so much in our world that it takes a new perspective to apply simpler strategies and techniques for a truly brilliant breakthrough. Mr.

Silverburg has quite a knack for that perspective. His rigging technique will be applied to the next ship built by ROSE and should cut manpower need in half. We'll just have to work on the name."

"Told you!" Missy spat at Rube. "So what's the proposal then?" she asked Lord Fearing.

"I want the two of you to be enrolled at ROSE Academy immediately. You are a few years behind other students your age, but I think you are both brilliant enough to catch up and excel."

Missy could feel her lower jaw hit her chest as she sat back up in bed. "What? How? We aren't nobles. We can't join ROSE."

"Technically," her father chimed in, "you are a noble."

"Not that anyone outside this room knows that!" Missy cried. "Or that I even knew it for sure until like ten minutes ago."

Lord Fearing laughed. "I can take care of that, Miss Beechworth. Mr. Silverburg has earned his place by winning the Inventionfest Open. We fully intended to offer Academy placement to any truly brilliant teenager that competed anyway. As for you? Even in your adoptive family you still have claims to nobility."

Missy's head snapped to the diminutive toymaker. He grinned sheepishly. "You're a noble? Why do you make toys for a living and struggle to pay your bills?"

"I am happier doing that. I am happier in Scraptown than The Reach," was all Simon Beechworth answered.

Missy saw in his eyes that no further explanation was needed.

"I told you we were old friends," Lord Fearing said with a smile. "The Beechworth family may not be as famous as the Hawtrey or von Deutsch families, but they are old and respected. Simon struck out on his own long ago but never legally relinquished his claim to nobility. He just chose not to act on it. Now he can, for your sake." Lord Fearing looked at Simon with a special twinkle in the gold-monocle covered eye.

Missy looked around the room and felt her head swimming with all the new information being dropped on her so shortly after waking up from electrocution. These nobles really knew how to get into your head and spin you around. She locked eyes with Rube, who smiled and nodded to her. So Rube had already decided.

"Can I make a counter proposal?" Missy asked.

Lord Fearing's monocle rose along with his eyebrows. "Oh? Getting to attend ROSE Academy isn't enough of an offer for you?"

Missy shook her head. "I only wanted to win the Inventionfest for the prize money so I could get my father out of debt. ROSE has more money than anyone. Can you guys make sure his debt is clear so he can continue to keep the toyshop open?"

This time the leader of ROSE raised his monocle with a smile instead of his eyes. "I think we can take care of that, Miss Beechworth. Do you accept my invitation?"

She looked at Lord Fearing, Rube, then her father in turn. "Papa?" she questioned.

"Yes, Misa?" he asked in return.

"What do you think?"

"It's your decision. You can follow in your real father's footsteps into ROSE and get to use that amazing brain of yours for more than tinkering and scavenging."

Missy scoffed.

"You don't agree?" Simon asked.

She laughed. "I agree with the amazing brain part. I disagree with the 'real father' part. Darnell Hawtrey may be my father by blood, but you are my Papa. I'd rather follow in your footsteps than his."

Simon Beechworth, who always had a smile on his face, added a little glisten to his eyes as he looked at his daughter. "All the more reason to bring your brain and your heart to that stuffy academy." He paused and looked at Lord Fearing. "No offense, old friend."

Lord Fearing simply grinned and pointed to his golden monocle then his top hat. "It's a fair point, Simon."

Missy shook her head at the strange exchange between Lord Fearing and her father. Then she made up her mind and said, "Let's do it. I'm in."

Lord Fearing nodded. "I'm happy to hear it, Miss Beechworth. I can't say it will be an easy transition for you two, but while you may not have the upbringing of nobles, you have the spirit of what ROSE was created for in the beginning in you. Now," he said with a pause, "one last order of business to clear up before I get on my way." He put his fingers to his mouth and whistled.

A door opened at the far side of the room and one last familiar face joined the congregation. Heinrich von Deutsch stood at the entrance to the hospital room, tall and strong, but somehow small and sheepish at the same time. "Hello, Miss Beechworth. Mr. Silverburg. Mr. Beechworth."

"What's von Douche doing here?" Missy asked.

"He'll be your liaison to ROSE Academy. As an upper year student and one of our best ambassadors, I felt he would be a good fit for helping you two adjust. Considering the adventure you all had together in the Dustwaste Wellspring, I figured you'd have more in common with him than any of the other students."

"Is he going to take credit for all of our test scores too?" Rube called out mockingly.

"I didn't take credit for anything," Heinrich said defensively.

"Oh, really? That's not the story we lesser people heard in Scraptown," Missy replied.

"Mr. von Deutsch is telling the truth," Lord Fearing intervened. "His report upon returning with *The Indefatigable* gave a full account of how important both of you were to both survival and making it home safely. He even admitted that it was his fault in the first place that the three of you ended up stranded out there. His father, however, didn't like that version of the narrative."

"So you just let him control the story?" Missy asked.

"Being the leader of ROSE doesn't make me all powerful, Miss Beechworth. Hans von Deutsch is a resourceful man. In fact, he doesn't even know Heinrich reported to me before he even debriefed his father. I'm sorry that the real story of your heroics can't be out there, at least for now, but I have a feeling you'll make an even bigger impact than returning an old airship to us."

"Oh?"

Lord Fearing pointed to the mechanical cat, whirring a purr on Simon Beechworth's lap. "I truly hope you'll continue working on that nanomotor. As a

ROSE Academy student, you'll have our full support to work with Hawtrey's iridium and maybe even help us learn more about it."

Missy felt her mouth open for the second time during this conversation. She closed it and said, "You're going to let me keep it?"

Lord Fearing held a finger to his lips. "Our little secret, Miss Beechworth. So long as you report to me directly on your research. As far as I can tell from Master von Deutsch's story and your own admissions to Metallurgist Winthrop and Baron Bjorn, that small piece of metal kept an entire airship afloat well after you all should have ran out of fuel and fallen. I'd love to see what you could do with it."

Missy smiled and reached over to grab Sprocket from her father. She smiled at her dad, her best friend, the head of ROSE, and even Heinrich. "Are you sure about this, Lord Fearing?"

"About what?"

"Are you sure ROSE Academy is ready for Misanthrope Beechworth?"

Lord Fearing laughed. "I am sure they are not, Miss Beechworth. And I can't wait to see it."

Missy petted her cat and imagined the tiny nanomotor inside with the small piece of iridium that may or may not be infected with alien bacteria. She couldn't wait to start the next phase of her life. It was scary and exciting and she still had more questions than answers. But at least now she had a future that didn't consist of simply trying not to die on a scavenging mission before she turned twenty. And that was something.

About the Author

Author Photo By Samantha Rodden

Jeremy Rodden holds a Bachelor's degree in Religion and English Writing from La Salle University and a Master's in Education from Holy Family University. He worked briefly as a High School English teacher before becoming a full-time stay-at-home dad and author.

Follow his blog and learn more about the author and his works at www.toonopolis.com. He can also be found being active on Facebook (www.facebook.com/toonopolisfiles/) or Twitter (www.twitter.com/toonopolis).

Other Works by Jeremy Rodden

Toonopolis: Gemini (*Toonopolis Files*, #1)

Toonopolis: Chi Lin (*Toonopolis Files*, #2)

The Myth of Mr. Mom: Real Stories by Real Stay-At-Home Dads

Anthologies Containing Toonopolis Stories

A World of Their Own (short story, flash fiction)

UnCommon Lands (Ao [adult section of the Tooniverse] short story)

Demonic Wildlife (short story)

Demonic Household (short story)

Anthologies Containing Non-Toonopolis Stories

UnCommon Evil (thriller/horror short story)

Brave New Girls: Tales of Heroines Who Hack (cyberpunk short story)

Paws, Claws, & Magic Tales (cat-themed short story)

Fae Thee Well (fairy tale retelling short story)

Toonopolis: Gemini
Sample Chapters

Prologue

Agent Log: Project Gemini

Entry Number: 1

Date: April 15

When I first returned from my trip to Toonopolis, I found it hard to put into words what I had experienced. I worried that the story about my time in the cartoon world would be seen, at best, as an excuse for failing a mission; at worst, as the rambling delusions of an agent who had lost his mind.

To this day, I still struggle when trying to explain my experiences. Fortunately for me, my superiors were not men to dismiss extraordinary tales easily, and my track record with the Agency was otherwise pristine. I reported to those stoic men just as I had done thousands of times before-specific, detailed, chronological, and truthful.

At first, I simply hoped they believed me. After I completed my report, my feelings shifted to a hope that they wouldn't have me exterminated as an insane liability. If it were not for the possibility that this avenue might open doors to a new realm of opportunity for the Agency, they probably would have. I am just lucky that they were willing to take risks.

Based on my report, they funded Project Gemini. After initially fearing that my life was in jeopardy, I found myself leading a venture for the Agency that placed us at the genesis of a new era of covert operations.

Prologue

The Agency spent millions of dollars and thousands of man-hours in the attempt to recreate the conditions that led to my entrance into the cartoon world, the Tooniverse, as the natives called it. It wasn't until we tapped into the resources of our neurology division that we realized we already possessed the requisite knowledge.

Though he didn't know it at the time, renowned neuroscientist Dr. James Robert Grenk had already discovered the process that could send someone into the Tooniverse. His research into a pain disorder known as RSD gave us the key, and his family yielded us a keymaster in his sixteen-year-old son. Jacob Grenk is a perfect test subject for us-intelligent, creative, and antisocial. Aside from his father, Jacob has no real meaningful connections to anyone.

Toonopolis: Gemini

After a year of research, development, and preparation, we are finally prepared to show my superiors that their judgment was not lacking and their trust in me was well-placed. Today we send a human consciousness into the Tooniverse to do our bidding.

Special Agent Mimic

April 15

Chapter One

Field Of Dreams

A teenage boy suddenly appeared in a field, his brow wrinkled in confusion. He was definitely stunned. In his left ear, he heard a faint popping sound followed by a slight whoosh of air as if an untied balloon had been released.

He unsuccessfully tried to remember anything prior to finding himself seated in this grassy field. He felt lost and confused and he realized that he was sitting down. He stood up, straightened his glasses, then brushed the clinging grass and dirt from his pants, and rubbed his hands together to remove the rest of the debris. He gazed around but could see nothing save the wide-open field in front of him.

It was a fortunate coincidence that an antique-style, full-length mirror walked up to him at that instant. The mirror gave him a full view of his reflection, even though he didn't recognize the boy he saw, a teenager, no more than fifteen or sixteen, with short unruly red hair and black horn-rimmed glasses. Freckles dotted his cheeks just below his cloudless blue eyes. The boy brought his pale, skinny arms to his face to ensure that he could feel what he was seeing and to confirm that it truly was his own image in the mirror.

He observed the gaudy clothes he was wearing—a lime green t-shirt and fuchsia cargo pants. He quickly recalled that the mirror in which he was examining himself had *walked* up to him. Even in his disoriented state of mind, he knew that mirrors couldn't just walk around wherever they wanted. At least, he thought he knew that.

"Hello?" the teenager said to the person he presumed was holding the mirror. He attempted to walk around to the back of the looking glass to see who was quietly taunting him. The mirror, though, spun with him to keep the reflective surface facing forward. "This isn't very funny, you know," the boy said

Much to the young man's surprise, the top portion of the mirror opened like a mouth and responded, "It also isn't very funny to try to look at someone else's butt without at least introducing yourself first." The looking glass emphasized its apparent disgust with a firm nod of the top of its frame.

"How are you doing that?" asked the boy, still trying to look behind the tall mirror.

"Well, if you are that interested in my backside, fine!" the mirror said in annoyance. It turned around, giving the red-haired boy a full view of a dark wooden backboard, such as one would expect to see on the reverse side of a tall looking glass. The mirror turned back around. "Are you satisfied?" it asked. Then it turned its back toward the bewildered boy again and began walking away on its very tiny legs.

The teenager looked down at his hands and back up to the mirror that was hobbling away as fast as its short legs would allow. "Wait," the boy whimpered quietly without really expecting the mirror to hear him. He had a million questions running through his mind but was unable to vocalize any of them. He paused to take an inventory of what information he had to work with to figure out where he was.

Before he could begin, the mirror was back in his face, showing the boy how much his forehead was crimpled in confusion. "Wait for what?" the looking glass asked, tapping one of its legs impatiently.

"Where am I?" was the question that jumped out of the boy's mouth. He didn't even have time to wonder how the mirror could hear him since it had no discernible ears.

"How should I know?" the mirror retorted. "I'm just an antique looking glass."

The young man suddenly had an idea inspired by a story from his childhood about a young girl who, like himself, found herself in a strange land full of bewilderment. It was with this thought in mind that he decided to run headfirst into the mirror. A loud *thud* and his rump landing on the grass were all he earned for his bright idea.

"Ow!" shouted the mirror. "What in the world did you do that for?"

"I guess I can't travel through you, huh?" The boy rubbed his head. He rose to his feet gingerly.

"I'm not sure why you thought you could. If you're quite done, I'd like to be on my way."

"On your way where?"

The boy thought he could make out annoyance in the upper frame of the looking glass, but he still couldn't figure out how it spoke. "Why, to Toonopolis, of course! It's where all of us begin our journeys."

The mirror spoke as though it was common knowledge. The young man wrinkled his brow with a grimace that clearly showed his ignorance of this information. "What is your name?" asked the mirror.

"I don't know."

"What an ill-formed thought you are," the mirror began. "You don't recall anything of your name or who you are?"

There was what seemed like a long pause as the boy struggled to come up with something that might be his name. He had plenty of vague memories floating in his mind, like the one about the girl and the looking glass, but to him it seemed that the only real existence he had ever known began moments ago when he became aware that he was sitting down in a field.

Only one word seemed to be a common thread in all of the jumbled memories that he was not sure were even his own. "Gemini," he said more to himself than to the mirror still standing impatiently in front of him.

"That's your name, kid? Gemini?"

"Kid . . . Gemini?" he mumbled, still mulling through his murky mind.

"Well, Kid Gemini—"

"No, just Gemini."

"Okay, Gemini," the annoyed mirror said. "I'm on my way to the big city. You can sit here and look dumb all you want, but I've got things to view and people to, er, view themselves." The mirror wobble-walked itself away from the boy.

"Gemini," he said out loud to test the name on his own ears. He wasn't entirely sure it actually was his name, as it did not sound very real to him. Then again, he thought, it was about as real as a walking, talking, standing mirror.

He decided to accept Gemini as his moniker. He felt good to have at least come up with a name for himself. The name alone did not, however, come close to answering the question of who he was, how he ended up in this strange field, or why he didn't clearly remember anything before the field.

While thinking about what he didn't know, the boy looked over the top of the retreating mirror and saw the large city on the horizon. As his gaze swept over the completely foreign city skyline, his eyes fell on the sun overlooking it.

Normally, the phrase "sun overlooking" would be an overused personification. In this case, however, the yellow-orange sun that Gemini was staring at actually had eyes and was quite literally looking at the city. Feeling the heat of Gemini's gaze, the sun turned its attention to the lone figure standing in the grass.

Gemini suddenly felt very small. When the sun winked at him, he nearly passed out. Gemini gaped at the cartoonish sun until the large ball of gas lost interest and turned its attention back toward the city. Gemini followed the sun's lead and also looked at the city skyline.

Field of Dreams

While there were some elements that reminded him of cityscapes he knew he had seen somewhere else before, there were also elements that reminded him of nothing he had seen before. He was not sure if it was because the city seemed so odd or if it was because his memory was so hazy.

Gemini saw tall skyscrapers made of glass, metal, wood, stone, and countless other materials, and could have sworn that one large building resembled a papier-mâché piñata. There also were numerous statues and monuments, some of which resembled ones he knew existed in other places. Some were completely new to him.

It was most difficult trying to absorb the vast diversity of the city he was looking at because it was constantly changing. Buildings were switching places, some of the monuments completely vanished only to be replaced by something new, and several of the buildings were changing colors, sizes, and even the construction materials right before his very eyes.

Gemini stood in the field trying to take in all he saw. He realized that he could not see an end to the city in either direction. The entire horizon at the edge of the field was covered with this shifting, varied cityscape.

"What is that?" he wondered aloud.

A loud popping sound next to him distracted Gemini. He turned toward the sound to find a large creature that appeared to be a cross between a kangaroo and a duck standing in a previously unoccupied space. The kangaroo-duck was wearing a yellow vest, a yellow sombrero, and nothing else. The creature looked like a five-year-old had drawn it.

"Hello?" Gemini ventured.

"Hola con queso!" screamed the kangaroo-duck and sprinted toward the city. After about fifty yards, the kangaroo-duck suddenly disappeared, leaving Gemini scratching his head and wondering if stranger things were even possible at this point.

Not knowing what else to do, he started walking toward the ever-changing city in the distance. As Gemini walked in the open field, he became aware of a path that he was fairly certain was not there when he began.

The rainbow-colored walkway was made of oddly shaped rectangular rocks with rounded edges. Or so he thought. He knelt down for a closer inspection and found the pathway to be made of a plethora of PEZ candies.

"Follow the Rainbow-PEZ Road," said a cheery voice behind him.

Gemini turned and discovered a being that resembled a garden gnome, who was smiling at him. The teenager thought his own fuchsia and lime clothing was gaudy, but the gnome made Gemini's clothes look plain in comparison. He was decked head to toe in rainbow-colored clothing including a giant bow tie and a pointy hat that looked like an old-school dunce cap.

"And who are you?" asked Gemini.

"My name is Roy," answered the gnome, his smile never faltering. "And you are?"

"Confused."

"Well, nice to meet you, Confused."

"No, my name isn't Confused. I'm confused."

Roy continued to smile, but his eyes narrowed a little. "Well, now I'm confused."

Gemini slapped himself in the face and groaned. "My name is Gemini. I am confused because I don't know what is going on and all of a sudden I find myself standing in a strange field talking to a garden gnome dressed in rainbows."

"Ah," said Roy, "I can see how that could be confusing."

Gemini sighed and stepped onto the Rainbow-PEZ Road with a loud crunch as the miniscule candy bricks crumbled under his sneakers. A wooden sign popped up in front of him as soon as his feet touched the road. He looked at Roy, who was still wearing a beaming smile.

"And which way should I follow this road?" asked Gemini.

"Read the sign," said Roy, the smiling gnome.

Gemini looked at the sign, which had a crudely drawn arrow on it pointing toward the large city at the end of the field and words written above the arrow: Toonopolis – 202,752 PEZes northeast. Just below that direction was an arrow pointing away from the road with the following words: Field of Dreams – 0 PEZes that-a-way.

Thanks to the timely intrusion of the magically appearing sign and Roy the gnome's encouragement, Gemini knew that the city he was walking toward was the same Toonopolis mentioned earlier by the mirror whose name he failed to catch.

"Well, I hope you learn a lot! Maybe we'll meet again one day!" Roy called out with more optimism than Gemini felt was healthy. He then vanished in an explosion of color that made Gemini shield his eyes.

Gemini turned away from the spot where the gnome had been standing and began his crunching, PEZ-dust-creating trek toward the city in the distance. He eyed the Rainbow-PEZ Road as it cut a colorful line in the otherwise plain green field around him.

He moved closer to Toonopolis, occasionally picking up handfuls of PEZ to eat along the way. He could only imagine what would await him inside the city limits. Gemini munched on the road and he knew his journey was bound to get even more interesting before he had any answers to who he really was and why he was in this weird place.